2   F

JUST IMAGINE

JUST IMAGINE

PAT LOWERY COLLINS

Houghton Mifflin Company
Boston 2001

I'd like to thank my editor, Margaret Raymo, for her amazing eye
for every detail and her unerring instincts for the needs of
the book as a whole. Her respect for my words and vision
and her careful editing are deeply appreciated.

Copyright © 2001 by Pat Lowery Collins

www.houghtonmifflinbooks.com

The text of this book is set in 12-point Aldine.

Library of Congress Cataloging-in-Publication Data

Collins, Pat Lowery.
Just imagine / Pat Lowery Collins.
p. cm.
Summary: During the Depression, having discovered that she has the ability to
have out-of-body experiences, twelve-year-old Mary Francis tries to use it to deal
with the "peculiar domestic situation" caused by her family's financial plight.
ISBN 0-618-05603-3
[1. Astral projection—Fiction. 2. Family life—Fiction.
3. Depressions—1929—Fiction.] I. Title.

PZ7.C69675 Ju 2001
[Fic]—dc21

00-033464

Manufactured in the United States of America

QUM 10 9 8 7 6 5 4 3 2 1

For my parents,
Margaret and Joseph Lowery,
who were inseparable.

CHAPTER ONE

IF IT HADN'T BEEN FOR NORA, IF SHE HADN'T SEEN THE possibilities in me, perhaps I'd have been as unaware of my gift as Mama sometimes was of hers. It was pretty clear to me that she could tell the future, but Gram always said that anyone who made so many wild guesses was bound to get lucky once in a while.

For as long as I could remember, Nora, the spiritualist minister in the family, visited from time to time as we moved from one town to another around Los Angeles —Leimert Park, Culver City, Hawthorne— before Mama found the big house in Beverly Hills. It turned out that what Mama had been looking for all along was something movie-starrish with a tiled roof and a patio and a big yard, a place that none of the other relatives from Michigan, sprinkled around L.A. like avocado trees, could afford. The only reason we could buy it was because it was the Depression and because the house had been foreclosed on and auctioned off. Mama had just been waiting for a deal like this one and was willing to overlook a few things, like an overgrown back yard and a kitchen as narrow as an alley. Of course, what really made the whole thing possible was that my daddy had a steady job as a local business manager for the WPA that Mama called "Depression proof" and Gram had her insurance payments.

Mama liked the way everybody was intimidated now and didn't drop in anymore but waited to be invited. When she did expect company, she'd be after me for days to clean my room and, since he was such a little kid, I'd help Leland clean his. Gram would bake non-stop, and Daddy would smack the Adirondack chairs he'd made in his night school wood shop class right down between the two orange trees and the one lemon.

We'd been in our new house for about six months before Nora came to look it over. Just before she arrived, Mama took me aside to explain again, in case I hadn't understood before, I guess, that Nora was something like Aimee Semple McPherson, the lady preacher whose great round temple we passed every time we went to Echo Park to feed the ducks. Only Mama said Nora didn't do outrageous things like riding her bicycle out on the altar as Aimee once did, and, of course, Nora wasn't famous like her and she'd only had one husband. He, unfortunately, was Fred — a rough, perpetually sunburned man with fine wrinkles of exasperation framing his perfect, white-toothed smile. When Nora said anything, her words were like whiffs of smoke from spirit worlds; his seemed lifted from the tarpaper roofs he repaired as a trade, gravelly and often dirty.

I remember tea parties in Nora's yard the few times Mama and Gram took Leland and me along for a visit. Since it was understood we'd never be invited into her house for some reason, we'd make ourselves at home outside, running up and down the narrow paths through scraggly beds of giant dahlias, sunflowers, and tiger lilies. When we grew tired of this, and of playing hide-and-seek behind the clumps of bamboo, she'd serve tea on little tables in the shade of a catalpa tree and sit us down on stools as if we were her playmates instead of Mama's children. Mama and Gram sat in regular chairs, but Nora would giggle and heave her great big body onto the grass next to us. I appreciated this enormous effort to be at our level and did my best to help Mama and Gram pull her up when she was ready. Times like that, from the warm way she put a hand on my shoulder or patted my cheek, I felt she must be partial to me and that I'd really like to get to know her better. I had every intention of doing it someday and couldn't have known that there was any hurry. When I did understand, it was too late, and I felt cheated.

The day Nora and Fred drove up to our house in his roofing truck with REPAIR YOUR ROOF WITHOUT A RUCKUS painted on the side, they both fussed a lot about the long drive from Huntington Park and how hard it had been to find us.

"Of course, we was looking for you north of Sunset," Fred muttered. "Who would have thought it was still

Beverly Hills so close to Santa Monica Boulevard."

Nora stared in amazement at the glass portico above the entrance and stumbled a little going up the steps. I remember being astonished all over again at how fat she was and how Fred had to steer her along, and I remember thinking how she probably couldn't have ridden a bicycle even if she'd wanted to. Leland gazed up at them both, his mouth gaping so wide that Fred said he could see his tonsils.

"The child has no tonsils," said Gram, snapping Leland's lips shut with one hand and shooing him off. She all but snorted. "His mama had his perfectly good ones removed to improve his singing."

"Now, Ma," Mama said sweetly, "You know perfectly well Leland's little tonsils were diseased. Why, he used to come down with tonsillitis each and every time I no more than turned my back."

I have another memory of Nora, wearing a black robe and striding across a small stage. Because I was never allowed to attend her church, I know that this memory must be rooted in imagination, yet it's as vivid as the reality of her speckled dress that day she came to visit and the way it cascaded from one round part of her to another and fluttered over her thick calves.

She was related to my grandmother in some remote way that was never explained. I think, though, that she must have been from the side of Gram's family that had moved from Michigan to California about the same time my parents had, before I was born. And no one told me how she came to found her own religion when every other relative was Roman Catholic, forbidden by some church law even to see her preach. Although Mama hadn't seen the performance either, she said that someone had told her how Nora had "out-of-body" experiences right there on stage, her spirit rushing off unseen somewhere, her body just staying put. She talked about Nora's trips as if they were absolutely true, and she and Gram wondered aloud things like, "Why do you suppose she keeps going into the body of that big black woman she calls Lillian the way she says?" and "Where in the world does the spirit of that poor woman go?" They often carried on whole conversations about it by bouncing questions back and forth. I decided that Lillian must be dark as night or they would have called her colored like they did the lady who came on Wednesdays to iron. Did Lillian and Nora exchange places?

"They say Nora's body doesn't move at all after the spirit leaves her," Mama told us once. "They say she shakes and lurches a little bit right before. But then she's like some great big guardian angel up on that stage. She hardly even breathes."

Without anything else to go on, I used to imagine Nora in her minister's robes. I'd envision her expressions as she took her trances and left the body in front of all the followers who could fit into the one-room church Fred had added onto their stucco bungalow himself. Mama said a door led from the dining room right to the stage, and I pictured Nora getting up from dinner and walking out there, filling the space that had no altar. It probably smelled of new wood and the varnish Daddy sometimes put on things he made in wood shop class. I could just see that roomful of people trying not to slip down on those slick seats, could see them watching her and the dumfounded looks on every one of their faces. And she never paused when I thought about her but made some announcements (I figured she'd have some novenas scheduled or something) and went right on with separating herself, her spirit, from all that flesh, leaving everyone behind, open-mouthed.

When Nora arrived at our new house, Mama swooped to the door like a bird, her "Hello! Hello! Hello!" floating across our wide new lawn and into the trees. It embarrassed me when she met people at the door this way. I wanted to put a bit between her teeth, like the ones horses wore in Tom Mix movies, and rein her in.

But Nora smiled cautiously and continued to look around like she must be in the wrong place. Fred was the first one to say anything.

"Goddammit, Loreen. We knew you was gettin' a bigger place, but this one takes the cake!"

He slapped his leg and released a cloud of cigar

smoke from between his teeth. "That tile roof will give you trouble sooner or later, though. After a while, those things get real leaky."

Mama ignored him.

"Well, Nora. What do you think?" she asked.

"Suits you, Loreen," Nora said, but her lips pursed together as if about to suck back the few words she'd forced through them.

Gram was already putting dinner on the table as they came in the door. She stopped just long enough to say, "Sit right down now before it gets cold." They were invited for five and we would eat on the dot.

Nora looked uncomfortable on the high dining room chair, her thighs seeming to merge with the over-stuffed seat. But she relaxed as she noisily sucked a rabbit leg, leaving it bare as a stick.

"Chicken and rabbit are two things you just have to eat with your fingers," said Gram. "Ain't no other way."

We figured it was a signal for us to pick ours up, too, and Leland grabbed his piece and bit big chunks, looking straight at Mama.

"It's okay, Mary Francis," he whispered to me between bites. "Gram said it was okay."

But, to look more polite, I continued to stab at mine with a knife and fork and finally lost my appetite completely while keeping track of the rhythm Nora had going between filling her plate and stuffing herself. She hadn't hesitated once, and I was sure she was about to when Daddy said, "Pay attention to what's on your own plate, Mary Francis."

When I looked back at Nora next to Fred, both unaware of anything but their food, I couldn't help but think how that black woman, Lillian, must take up residence somewhere else. Sure as shootin' she'd want to avoid having anything to do with Fred. But how did Nora's spirit fit into the other lady's family? Did she even have a family? Was she childless like Fred and Nora or was there a baby for Nora to play with or a little six-year-old kid like Leland who she could pretend belonged to her? Did Lillian have a husband of her own? If she did, what was he like and did he notice the sudden changes in her?

They didn't stay long after the banana cream pie. Mama wanted to show off the garden, but Nora said she'd had an especially trying trip in and out of Lillian's body that same morning and needed to get to bed. I could certainly understand how she must feel when I learned that Lillian lived someplace just this side of San Francisco. I wondered how they'd ever gotten in touch with each other in the first place.

Gram started giving me shushing signals with her eyebrows when I asked Nora, "What was it like? Your trip, I mean?"

But Nora smiled broadly for the first time that day and sighed so loudly it was tuneful.

"I'm not sure you could understand, dear."

She passed the back of her hand across her forehead and looked away. Then she suddenly turned back to me and fixed me to the spot with her dark, flashing pupils.

"Unless of course you are one of the few, one of the gifted."

She continued to glare at me, not unkindly, but as though I were a piece of cloth and she wanted to make sure I wouldn't shrink up in the wash.

She's reading my mind, I thought.

"Loreen," she said, still considering me but talking to Mama. "I think she may have it after all. I always felt there was something unusual about this child. Didn't I always say how I felt that, Fred?"

She sat down again. The mind reading had taken its toll. She was breathing heavily.

"Hell, Nora. Don't get all excited," Fred said. "She's just a little kid."

"I'm already twelve," I said.

"And she's Catholic," my father said.

But Mama ignored them both. "You could be right, Nora. Of course we've always considered darling little Leland to be the one with the talent, the way he dances and sings even better than Shirley Temple. But Mary Francis has this very sensitive nature."

"Oh, for Pete's sake!" It was as close to swearing as my father ever got, and Mama backed off.

"Don't fret yourself," said Gram, helping Nora to

her feet. She looked for all the world like a mouse boosting a sow. "Seems to me a gift like that wouldn't likely skip a generation. I mean, it clearly ignored my Forest completely."

"You never can tell," said Nora earnestly, and those were the words I kept hearing for days after she and Fred went back home.

CHAPTER TWO

I'D BEEN WORKING ON IT ONE WHOLE WEEK WITH NO luck. A few times there'd been this massive tingling all over, but that was after concentrating so hard my head hurt. It wasn't until I just got desperate and really let go that it happened. Actually, I had decided to keep all the hoping and wishing but to just stop thinking so hard. In fact, I had become completely lost in playing "Lady of Spain" on the accordion, when I suddenly saw that my fingers were moving across the keyboard effortlessly, mindlessly, for my mind hovered just about three quarters of the way up the wall, out-of-body, free. There had been a slight jolt that I'd pretty much ignored when going from one state to another, and the first time lasted only till right before the third page, when I snapped together just in time to turn the sheet music.

After that, I knew to empty my mind again and sort of float inside in order to take off. Then the jolt would be even less noticeable, and I could manage longer periods and higher elevations, getting closer to the chandelier every time. Any interruptions catapulted my soul toward my body in a frightening rush.

Thinking about the whole experience afterwards, it seemed completely right that it should be happening to me, and it felt just about how I'd expected it would.

I soon learned that if I picked a time to practice when Mama and Leland were at one of his lessons and Gram was out of the house or busy in the kitchen, I could enjoy a prolonged state of buoyancy that couldn't be described in physical terms. It was why, I could see now, Nora hadn't been able to explain it to me. Of course leaving behind a wiry body with scabby knees probably couldn't compare to the relief Nora must feel at shedding all those pounds, her painful bunion, and her famous migraine headaches. But there was a wonderful feeling of sharing something unique, even if she didn't know anything about it. Someday we would sit down and compare notes — maybe have one of those tea parties — for I was certain that these start-up experiences would escalate into the trips through time and space that Nora told her congregation about.

Though Mama didn't notice how much my playing improved when I let my mind take off, Gram did. One day, in fact, she stopped me on my way to school and showed me a news clipping of a girl on roller skates apparently zipping back and forth across a stage and all the while playing her accordion like crazy — fingers, limbs, and hair flying.

"Just imagine! I'll bet you could do that if you tried hard enough!" she said with a tilted smile that implied this was the kind of thing to make Hollywood sit up and notice. Gram seemed to hope as much as I did, sometimes, that I'd discover a talent of my own that would make Mama want to put me in the movies, too. She said it was only fair. "I'm sure you could."

I took the clipping. Of course I could. And more! The girl pictured was awkward and plain and, judging from her peculiar pose, hadn't taken dancing lessons either. What I had in mind would be sure to get Mama's attention. In one magnificent flash, I saw myself skating out from Nora's dining room with graceful movements that connected perfectly with the sadly beautiful "Blue Danube Waltz." (It was one of the records that came with the Victrola Mama bought from a lady down the street from where we used to live. Leland danced to a more modern phonograph that Mama didn't want anyone but her to touch.) Then the jolt of separation, the uplifting of my musical artistry to a level never before achieved by a twelve-year-old girl. My picture would be in magazines in color, my spirit on its way out, a fleecy pink streak across the photograph.

I began to practice roller skating on the cracked cement driveway, avoiding the bump at the end that had once sent me hurtling into the street. After a few weeks I could do very shallow jumps and stick my leg out like Sonja Henie on ice. There was no way to find out if it was going to work with my accordion, though, because Mama had forbidden me in no uncertain terms to take it outside. I didn't get it. She let Leland tap dance all over the place.

And something would have to be done about the rusty skates I'd inherited from her. The girl in the picture clearly had on white shoe-boot ones.

"You know we can't afford things like that right now," Mama said when I asked, "what with Leland's costumes and all the little extras you always need when you set up a new house."

What about *my* costumes, or at least what about skates that looked like skates?

"It's a crazy notion, anyway," said Mama. "Who's gonna want to see a big girl like you careening around on skates and hefting a great big accordion like that?"

"I don't careen, Mama!" I pleaded. "It's like dancing. I dance."

"Some dance," said Daddy.

"And I levitate," I said quietly, even though I wasn't completely sure if that was the name for it (and it turned out later that it wasn't).

"You what?"

"I levitate."

"Where in the world did you pick up a big, meaningless word like *levitate*?" asked Daddy. "Nobody can do that. Nobody does it, do you hear? Not so-called psychics. Not some Indian whirling dervish. Not Nora. And certainly not little girls."

"I'm not a little girl."

14

"When you don't talk sense you are. If you want people to pay attention, if you want them to think you're grown up, you can't go around telling people you levitate."

"All right, I won't tell them. I'll keep it a secret," I said.

Daddy threatened me with the back of his hand.

"And don't sass me back, Mary Francis. Loreen," he said, calling Mama from the kitchen, "talk some sense into this child. You're the one said she had this very sensitive nature and made her think she had some out-of-this-world gift! You and Ma are responsible for her shenanigans and big ideas."

But Mr. Maloney, my newest accordion teacher, was aware of something. I was sure of it. Since we'd moved from East L.A. he still came to our house to give me lessons. It was at least twice as far for him as before, and for just one dollar and his dinner, it seemed a long way to come. Mama said it was because he'd grown fond of the family; Gram thought it was because of her floating island and apple Betty desserts, but it seemed to me that he must have finally discovered that same spark in me that Gram had noticed.

I'd seen a picture of him with his band when they'd played on the Cunard cruise ship to Hawaii. The Cunard logo was on a curtain behind them and there were a lot of dancing couples in party hats.

"See, Forest," Mama had said when she'd shown it

to Daddy, "he's not just a teacher. He's a real musician. Maybe she can really learn something this time."

The men in the band had on white coats and looked like a bunch of waiters. You could just see the pointed toes of Mr. Maloney's black-and-white wingtips. He was younger then, and his hair was slicked back. Now it had some gray in it, and his mustache was a funny orange color, as though he'd borrowed it from someone else. It always scratched my ear when he bent over me to arrange my hands on the keyboard.

"And he's always hugging me," I complained to Mama. It didn't matter that I was in the middle of a piece of music. He'd throw his arms around me and squeeze while I'd try to continue as if these interruptions were part of the lesson.

"Try to understand," Mama said. "He lost his little boy a few years ago. He'd have been just about your age. Mr. Maloney's still overcome with grief."

I knew *lost* didn't mean *misplaced*. It was like *passed away*. It meant *dead*, but no one ever said that word.

He showed me a picture of his son once. He had dark hair and wore a sailor suit. He didn't look anything like me. So this was a dead boy. Or at least he was going to be a dead boy. He couldn't have known when the picture was taken that that's what he would be. Now when I wanted to shove Mr. Maloney away, I felt terrible.

"Be polite," Mama would whisper right before he'd come into the room.

I didn't think I could be, but thanks to Nora, there was another solution, although the first time I tried separating from my body in Mr. Maloney's presence, it felt like jumpy starts in a broken car at the fun house. I hadn't yet tried it when anyone else was around and just couldn't let myself go. I kept clearing my throat and starting the *William Tell* overture again and again until Mr. Maloney began to tap his fingers on Mama's piano. But after about the fourth attempt, and with the help of some invisible force that I'd noticed before that was something like the wind or maybe like the earth breathing really hard, I could sense myself taking off. It was much easier after that. He plastered gold stars one after another into my lesson book and told Mama he was absolutely astonished at my progress.

This will do it, I thought. *This will convince Mama to get me an audition instead of Leland.* Because he was small for his age, had curly hair, and could dance and sing like crazy, she was sure he was going to be a big star.

"A little boy Shirley Temple," she liked to tell people. "He's gonna be our ticket to fame and fortune."

I probably should have said that I wanted an audition "too" not "instead," because I really didn't want to take anything away from Leland. He was the best kid in the world, so good sometimes it almost made you feel bad. And with his talent and good looks, he could be a movie star easy. I had no doubts about that. I just wanted a chance of my own. And sometimes I wished for his own sake that he'd go off and have more fun — you know, climb trees and catch frogs and play ball. But Mama didn't leave him much time to do things like that.

As for me, after weeks of spiritual hovering above my accordion, it suddenly seemed as though I was incapable of going any further. I was even losing ground, so to speak. One day I had been watching myself playing the Tarantella from above without any effort; the next, I was laboring over the keyboard, my fingers inching and stuttering along the keys. In fact, once, when I thought I must be rising out of reach of Mr. Maloney, I suddenly felt his prickly mustache against my ear and swatted it like a fly. Mr. Maloney bolted backwards and was caught by the curve of Mama's baby grand piano. I knew I'd been impolite and hoped he wouldn't tell her.

Of course, I didn't know yet about letting a talent grow, about starting out small, and much later, when I tried most of one whole afternoon, I seemed to have lost what I'd begun to think of as some kind of formula. It hadn't occurred to me that I was just trying too hard again. For the moment, there didn't seem to be any point in bothering with the roller skates.

It was what Gram called earthquake weather, hot and sticky with a few soggy dark clouds, the day I heard that Nora was sick. Mama and Gram were sitting at the breakfast room table talking about her illness as they talked daily about every addition to the flow of injured or sick acquaintances. I always listened to the way they dissected each diseased and broken part or considered the dead and dying. Gram's friend Mrs. Fisk had died and Mama and Gram didn't think God had made the right choice.

"She still had a lot of life in her. A short illness like that! You wouldn't think she'd go before poor Mr. Beaseley who's been suffering over a year now."

"You're right, Ma. He really should have taken old Mr. Beaseley. That man's just waiting to go. Mrs. Fisk has a daughter who loves her, and grandchildren . . ."

When the conversation switched back to the merely sick and I heard Nora's name, I couldn't believe it. Wasn't she above things like sickness? When it became clear from what they were saying that she really was sick, I could just see her, heaving silently under a massive sheet, her spirit resting behind closed eyelids, shutting out tiresome travel decisions. From the little I knew of spirits, at least of my own, they seemed to enjoy parts of everything — even bad things like headaches or fevers. For example, I liked to just lie there and watch the birds outside my window when I was sick and to feel like I was one of the flock when they flew off. And I loved any opportunity to listen to the daytime soap operas on the radio and to capture all the action inside my head. I supposed Nora's spirit might be enjoying some kind of vacation, too.

I thought about her on and off all through the day, when I wasn't wrestling with the feeling that something momentous like an earthquake was about to happen. I made sure all the cupboards were closed in the kitchen and took my blue willow tea set off the shelf of my closet so it couldn't fall. But the earth didn't shake. The next day was clear and dry and cloudless.

I wasn't at all prepared, however, for the abrupt announcement a week later that Nora had, in fact, passed away.

"Are you sure?" I asked Gram. "Is it an absolute fact?"

"Of course it's a fact. Would I go making up a thing like that?"

Had anyone been present for her final moments, I was certain they would have heard a tremendous *whoosh*, as the spirit, in peak form after an entire seven days of rest (just like God, I recollected), escaped to its final destination, wherever that was. I hoped if she was merely off in Europe or Africa this time, she'd have the sense to return before the closing of the coffin.

After the funeral, her church, whose only living minister now was Fred, immediately ceased to be. When later I heard the phrase "here today and gone tomorrow," I knew exactly what it meant. I was certain, though, that if anyone could make a return to earth after death, it would be Nora, and I waited to hear about it.

"Anybody heard from Nora?" I asked Mama one day when the suspense was really getting to me.

She looked at me as though I couldn't possibly belong to her.

"For heaven's sake, Mary Francis! Remember how I said that nobody, *nobody* ever comes back?" I was confused when she started to laugh. "Nora was no different than the rest of us when it comes to that."

I started looking in the newspaper, just in case. If she did make any contact, it would probably be in the headlines. LOCUSTS DEVOUR CROPS was the headline in both the *Los Angeles Times* and the *Beverly Hills Courier* the first day I looked. It was followed in a few days by SPEAKEASY SMASHED IN WEST L.A.

I soon found out that anything considered important enough for a headline had to do with the failing economy, Prohibition, or the problems in Europe, and I started looking through the rest of the paper in Special Events and even Local News. But after a while, when there were no testimonials or anything, and remembering that I'd only made it halfway up the wall and back myself, I suspected she'd exceeded her range this time.

Fred, alone, held as much interest for us as a minor character in a play. His words all on their own had lost any punch they might have had, and his once pungent profanities fell spongelike, soggy with their own lack of meaning. His infrequent visits stirred no curiosity, and we fed him with only a little more care than we did the vagrants who often came to the kitchen door at lunchtime. It turned out he was right about our roof, and we called him when it leaked or when a friend who had the money needed a roof repaired. He was Fred the roofer then, no longer the husband of Nora to those who knew her or the husband of the spiritualist minister to those who didn't.

That I had let the slight stir of Nora's talent in me slip away gnawed like a guilty secret. Though I wasn't sure yet how I'd do it, I was determined to get it back, to get it all back, to take it as far as I could go.

CHAPTER THREE

I COULDN'T DO ANYTHING ABOUT IT FOR A WHILE. I
mean, I would have tried, but the conditions weren't
even close to right. It was like anything else private, like
drawing or writing letters. With a big loud ruckus going
on all the time so you couldn't hear yourself think —
well, you couldn't. And you couldn't stop thinking and
really let go either.

In fact, I couldn't get much of anything done those
first few days after Daddy lost his job. Mama kept going
on about how we were bound to lose the house, too.
That was her biggest fear. Gram said that she'd known
there was going to be trouble as soon as we started getting too big for our britches and in over our heads. Of
course, we all knew she meant Mama and not the rest of
us, certainly not Daddy, her perfect boy.

But then he got another good job right away, something Mama said was unheard of in these hard times.
The trouble was, the job was clear across the country on
the eastern seaboard, which might just as well have
been the North Pole when Mama got to figuring out
how far it was from Hollywood and Leland's big break.

But she didn't want Daddy to turn it down. It was good money and you just didn't turn down a job like that in a depression, even though she couldn't see leaving her house behind or taking Leland away from what she called "this fertile field for his many talents."

"You can't have it both ways, Loreen," Daddy told her when she'd hashed and rehashed our dilemma so many times Gram and I had begun tuning her out. "Just put the house on the market and start packing."

He must have been getting desperate or he would have remembered that you didn't give Mama orders like that. She didn't take well to orders even when there were circumstances as special as right now.

Mama got really quiet. She looked at Daddy as if she'd suddenly decided not to have anything more to do with bald men or like he'd just told her we were going to rob a bank together. We all stayed quiet, too, and couldn't take our eyes off her and the way she was just looking at him like that.

"Well, it's plain to see," she said at last, "that my opinion doesn't count for much around here. 'Just start packing' you tell me, as if my life and all my dreams have got to revolve around you, as if you're the center of the universe."

"If by that you mean that I pay the bills," said Daddy, "you're darned tootin' I'm the center of the universe. If you want to take over in that capacity, be my guest. Just be my guest."

Gram got up and started banging pots around in the kitchen as if she didn't want to hear, and Leland sneaked out the back door. You could see him out there, hanging upside down on the jungle gym so long you'd think he'd get tired of all that blood in his head. But I didn't budge from my chair at the table, and it seemed they'd totally forgotten I was there. I sure as heck didn't want to miss anything they said. My future was at stake here as well as Mama's and Leland's. I didn't want her to mess it up for all of us.

But that was exactly what she seemed set on doing. Every word out of her mouth was digging a little grave for what we'd always called *family*. Every time Daddy tried to get her to settle down, tried to make her see what was clear as daylight to the rest of us, she'd flare up like some out-of-control bonfire and demand her rights.

It seems unbelievable to me that we were there at that table so long I finally fell asleep. But I can remember waking up in the middle of the night, still at the table with everybody else in bed and the house so quiet you could hear the air and feel some of the crackle left behind by all those words. When I walked down the hall to my bedroom and looked into Mama and Daddy's, there they were, each hugging a side of the bed to keep from touching. I wanted to pull them closer to each other, turn them over so their noses would meet. But instead I went into Leland's bedroom and pulled the covers up over his overalls. He must have put himself to bed.

In the morning everything seemed settled. It had to have happened after I fell asleep at the table, and I was sorry I'd missed it. But I wasn't happy with what Mama and Daddy had come up with. None of us was.

"We're gonna give this a try, Mary Francis," Daddy said as he buttered everybody's toast. "I'll run it by you, and you see what you think."

Of course, I knew it didn't matter what I thought, but I pretended that it did, and I listened.

"Mama's gonna stay here in this house with Leland for a while, just for a while, until he gets his big chance." He pushed a piece of toast at me and I took it. "And you and I and Gram will move back East." He was saying it like we'd been there before, like maybe we were on our way home or something.

Mama was smiling at him again. She wasn't saying a word. She was just smiling.

"Your Mama deserves this chance, you see. She's had all this faith in Leland all this time and he has this great big audition coming up."

She'd convinced him. Well, I wasn't surprised. But I didn't like this half-and-half business. Why was I going with Daddy and Gram? Why didn't Mama want me to stay with her? Why hadn't anyone asked me?

"It's a dumb idea," I said.

"It's nothing of the kind," said Mama. She leaned toward me as though we were going to share a secret. "And it's just for a while, Mary Francis." She winked at Daddy. "Why, you know I couldn't bear to be apart from Forest for too long."

When I'd first learned that my father had a name other than Daddy and that it was Forest, I wondered if he was named after a bunch of trees or if a bunch of trees was named after him. It seemed like a really important name either way. And I'd noticed that whenever Mama chose to use it in conversation, it was those times when he was doing exactly what she wanted. Like right now. Splitting us all up had been a dumb idea when she'd suggested it yesterday, and it was a dumb idea today. She wasn't going to get me to change my mind about that.

"Of course, I'd keep you with me," said Mama, "but you've got some serious schooling ahead of you. Why, high school is just around the corner, and we don't want to be yanking you in and out of schools like some yo-yo."

Was it the truth? Was that her real reason?

"I wouldn't mind, Mama. There are a couple of years before I'll have to worry about that. We'll all be back together in a couple of years."

"Well of course we will, dear. But your daddy and I think it'll be better this way for now. Gram and Daddy will need your help, and Leland and I will be making this great big push to get him started at last, to get the wheels turning for him."

She was making Leland sound like a broken old car instead of a cute little boy.

"And what if it doesn't work out for Leland?" asked Gram all of a sudden.

Mama shot her a real mean look.

"Tell your grandmother, Mary Francis, about my gift for seeing into the future, how I know just the way things are going to turn out before they even happen." She said it real sweetly, looking at me instead of Gram.

"She knows about that, Mama."

"I know she thinks that," said Gram. "But you couldn't prove it by me."

"Oh, well now," said Mama. "We wouldn't be anywhere at all if we were still waiting to prove things by you. The way you need some guarantee the sun will shine before you'll put your nose out the door, we'd still be in that leaky duplex in Leimert Park if we were waiting around to prove things by you."

"Well that might be a darned sight better than in over our heads in debt," said Gram. "And we wouldn't be having this conversation about where your duty lies."

Daddy got up and gave Mama a big smacky kiss on the top of her ear.

"Loreen knows where her duty lies, Ma. Make no mistake about that."

When Mama rolled her eyes at him and burrowed into his chest, Gram looked as if her arthritis had suddenly flared up. But I knew it was a pain of another kind, a thinking and feeling kind of pain that I'd grown accustomed to myself and that stabbed out of nowhere like that whenever Mama said or did things that affected all of us but didn't make good sense.

"I want to go with Mary Francis," said Leland, climbing into my lap. He took a big hank of my hair in one hand and twisted it around and around.

"Sure you do, honey," said Mama. "Sure you do. And we won't be on our own for very long at all."

"Why do I have to be a movie star?"

Mama laughed. "Oh, honey, don't say it as if you're being punished or something. When God sees fit to give somebody all that talent, well, He doesn't want that person to hide that light under a barrel."

"What does that mean?"

"It means you've got to share your talent with the whole world, that the whole world is waiting."

"For pity's sake," said Gram. "You'll have the child thinking he's the Messiah just because he knows how to dance and sing a little bit."

"You think this isn't going to be hard for me, too, Ma? Well, I surely won't miss your snide remarks. I won't miss those one little bit."

Was it going to be hard for Mama? She seemed so cheery when she wasn't talking to Gram that I couldn't help wondering. And the way she'd said "on our own" was like she'd been waiting for this chance all her life, as if this was just going to be one great big adventure for her and Leland.

"Stay here, Mary Francis," whined Leland. "You could be in the movies, too."

That was certainly the way I had thought about it before Mama had made me see the error of my ways. I almost didn't care about being in the movies anymore, but I did care about what Mama thought, even though I wished I didn't. I wanted her to think I was pretty and smart and talented, too. I wanted her to see me the way she'd seemed to that day when she'd bought me the blue felt hat. I hadn't even needed a hat, but she'd brought it home and placed it on my head like she was a milliner and I was a mannequin in a department store.

"There," she'd said with a wide smile at the hat after she'd gotten it just right. Her eyes slipped down then, over my face, as if she was seeing into *my* future for once. They smiled too.

"Looks like it belongs on top of some floozy," said Gram.

But you could tell Mama wasn't listening to her.

"I was absolutely right," she said. "When I saw that hat in the May Company window, I said to myself, that's what Mary Francis needs to look special. She needs a hat with pizzazz. She needs a blue hat the same color as her eyes."

The only hat I possessed till that day was the black beret I had for church, and I would never have thought to ask for a new one. But right away, without any practice at all, I did feel special in that blue hat, the way it fit close all around like the ones ladies wore. Just knowing it was up there on my head, I felt really different. Almost beautiful.

Now if I turned into somebody beautiful overnight, Mama wouldn't even know it, cause I'd be on the other side of the continental United States. Gram wouldn't notice it for sure. And Daddy wouldn't think to tell Mama about it even if he did notice.

CHAPTER FOUR

ALL OUR FURNITURE AND HOUSEHOLD STUFF WAS staying with Mama, so we didn't have much to take with us but our clothes. Except for Gram's extra pairs of orthopedic shoes, which she sent ahead by parcel post, everything fit into the big trunk of Daddy's Packard with room left over for the electric Singer sewing machine. Mama and Gram had words over who would keep that, with Mama asking how was she going to make Leland's handmade costumes without it and Gram telling her that Leland had too many costumes by half and the machine belonged to her. My accordion and the Victrola sat in the back seat with me and my blue hat. Even though the hat wasn't for summer, I wasn't squashing it into some valise.

Daddy had rented a furnished apartment in Hardenville, Massachusetts, sight unseen, saying how it would just be for a little while, so it didn't have to be perfect.

We traveled three hundred and fifty miles each and every day for about ten days to get there, stopping only for a bridge that had been washed away or hail storms or when a hose or tire blew. If we didn't come upon a cabin for rent somewhere before dark, we'd sometimes have to keep driving half the night in search of a place to stay.

When we found out that our new apartment didn't even come close to perfect, Daddy's great big hurry to get there seemed pretty misguided. What was waiting for us were five dingy rooms on the second floor of a triple-decker with a picture window that looked across to the biggest brick mill building you ever saw. It seemed to go on for miles in both directions, and it completely hid the river behind it.

"The real estate agent mentioned the river," said Daddy, looking like he might cry if it wasn't for the fact that he was a grown-up man, "but she didn't say a word about the mill."

"See," said Gram. "We should have taken that little detour to the Grand Canyon back at Flagstaff, Arizona." She was sitting on her suitcase in the tiny living room as if the dark brown Morris chairs that reeked of nicotine had fleas, too. "But no. You couldn't take that little fifty-mile detour. The one and only chance I'll probably ever have to see one of the Seven Wonders of the World, and you allowed it to pass me by."

She had begged to see Longwood Gardens in Pennsylvania, too, and I pleaded for a glimpse of the Liberty Bell in Philadelphia. But every time we asked Daddy to stop, even if it was just to see the tallest tree in Wisconsin or the fattest pig in Kansas, he'd remind us that this was no pleasure cruise. He even drove way around Boston so the historical sights of the Revolutionary War wouldn't tempt us. With all this time on my hands, I got so restless sometimes that I strongly considered making the effort again to free my spirit so it could explore the countryside on its own. The fact that I was so new at this — and that we were in a moving vehicle — stopped me. What if I couldn't make the connection when I wanted to return? My spirit might be floating around the buttes of New Mexico or the Iowa cornfields for all time to come.

The upshot of all our travel was that what Mama had told me would be an educational trip across our great land was nothing but a hot and boring race to the worst place we'd ever lived.

The gas stove leaked just enough so I could smell it, but Daddy couldn't. There was an icebox instead of the fancy new Frigidaire that we'd grown accustomed to in the Beverly Hills house, and the kitchen floor was some kind of pocked and stained old wood instead of shiny new linoleum.

"Why, this kitchen is worse than the one your grampa and I had when we was first married and lived in a cold-water flat in Evanston." Gram took off her shoe and swatted a bug. "And you don't find cockroaches like this in California. The climate is too ideal."

Though I didn't understand her logic, the bug she

was now scraping off her sole wasn't like any I had ever seen.

Then Gram and I learned we'd be sharing a room, the narrow back bedroom with bunk beds that seemed to be made out of some sort of twisted twigs, and we grappled with our desperation with completely different objections.

"It won't work." I said. "Gram can't climb up there on top, Daddy, and I'm too afraid of heights." That last part wasn't true, but I thought it might convince him.

"Mary Francis wouldn't get a wink of sleep with my reading lamp turned on at all hours. You know about my insomnia, Forest." She separated each syllable. "I can't room in with a growing girl who needs her sleep."

Daddy insisted there was no other way. There were only three bedrooms — one for him and Mama, one for Gram and me, and one for Leland.

When I wanted to know why a whole bedroom had to be saved for Leland, Daddy said, "Because of his masculine gender, Mary Francis," as if it was a perfectly good answer.

"But who knows when he and Mama are going to get here. That room might be empty for months."

In the end, Daddy agreed to let Gram sleep in there until Leland arrived, and I could sleep in the lower bed of twigs. It wasn't much of a victory, but it turned horrible into bearable at least temporarily. And it wasn't long before I noticed that if I slept backwards, with my feet where my head ought to be, I could get a glimpse of the New England woods out the one and only window. And since we could actually hear the river, the steady churn of it, I would imagine it was sweeping along a country road, rippling with sunlight and bubbling over rocks, until it might just as well have been visible. I liked the scenes I could paint in my head when I put my mind to it.

And after Gram cooked up some of her special soap and she and I started scrubbing and cleaning, the disgusting smell of cigarettes was covered up by the awful but familiar smell of her soap. She even soaked the upholstered furniture, then let it dry for days while we got used to sitting on the floor.

When Mrs. Feingold from downstairs came by one night with blintzes, we were able to sit down and eat them at the table just like we were what Gram called "civilized people."

"Such a nice little family," our new neighbor said, setting down the dish and looking around like she expected there'd be more of us. "Too many in these small apartments and you lose your mind. Take it from me. Before Mr. Feingold died and before my Joey joined the CCC boys, there wasn't room to turn around in our flat. My mother lives with me, you see. So that made four of us." She put her hands on her broad hips as if she was going to stick around and watch us eat. She nodded her broad face up and down in contented agreement with everything she'd just said.

"Oh, there'll be two more of us," said Daddy. "This is only temporary. A temporary solution until we buy a house."

"Buy a house!" exclaimed Mrs. Feingold as if it were some kind of dream she didn't believe. She seemed in a hurry now. "Well, enjoy the blintzes. Enjoy! Enjoy!"

She backed out the door and into Mrs. Krakas, the lady from upstairs who didn't look to be going anyplace; she'd just been standing outside our door and listening, I guess. Her baby carriage was always downstairs in the hall. I'd never seen her take it anywhere, though I'd seen the baby from a distance once or twice. Daddy said it was her footsteps or her husband's that I heard at night, pacing back and forth. He said the baby was probably a light sleeper. She cried a lot. The baby, I mean.

The one thing Daddy ran out and bought right away was a radio. And when Gram got her special programs back, especially the daytime ones like *Helen Trent,* and we could all tune in to *The Shadow* and *Fibber McGee* at night, things didn't seem quite so bad. It even drowned out the baby some of the time.

There were some kids who lived on our street, twin boys and some toddlers and a few girls younger than me who still played with dolls. The twins, Ike and Mike, were about my age and exactly alike—identically pale and identically near-sighted. Gram said their pallor was left over from New England winters and a bad diet. They had a language all their own that often left me out, but when they played kick the can and dodge ball in the street, they let me play sometimes, until I started winning.

Daddy's new job was as the business manager of a mill in the next town. Turned out there was a mill in just about every town around, though some of them were shut down and boarded up. So we probably couldn't have avoided looking at one no matter where we lived. I kept wondering what Mama would think if she saw this place, this apartment and this town. Sometimes I'd picture her walking into this very room, her mouth and eyes wide open with horror, and she wouldn't say a word. She'd just turn right around, pick Leland up, and take him straight back to Beverly Hills. It was why I didn't really tell her much when I wrote, none of the details. I was pretty sure Gram wouldn't even bother to write, and Daddy would keep trying to put a good face on things to get her to come and join us. They really were in love. I was sure of that. But sometimes, knowing what Mama wanted her life to be, I wasn't sure if they were in love enough. And she always said how much she loved me but, well, it hardly ever felt that way. It sure hadn't been enough to keep me by her side, no matter how I'd begged.

There was no school yet, no Leland to take care of,

nothing to do on days when Ike and Mike didn't let me play with them but help Gram a little bit and wander around. A few blocks away was a mom-and-pop store called LeGrande's, and Gram sent me there on a pretty regular basis to get stuff she'd forget to have Daddy pick up at the bigger market in town. She'd usually give me a nickel for a soda, and sometimes I'd save up for Buck Rogers comic books instead. I'd wait if they only had *Blondie* or *The Katzenjammer Kids*. Mr. LeGrande was tall and thin and Mrs. LeGrande was fat — plump, really, nice and plump. They made me think of Jack Sprat and his wife. They spoke French to each other and sometimes forgot and said things in French to me. They were pretty nice. They let me look through the comics as long as I wanted and didn't seem to mind if I didn't buy anything.

Because I had all this free time, I thought a lot about practicing my gift again, but I felt a little unsure about starting up in this strange new place and of the usefulness of such a trip at this particular time. I mean, Mama wasn't anywhere around to be impressed, Mr. Maloney was California history, and Gram was presently uninterested in any improvement in my musical skills.

One day I kept walking after I'd left LeGrande's and discovered the public library about a mile down the road. Gram told it to Daddy like this: "You'd think the child had found money in the street, the way she came back grinning ear to ear."

"It has a room full of books for kids," I wrote to Leland. And I told him he could have the top twig bunk when he got here. I was sure Daddy would never be able to get Gram out of the other bedroom now that her clothes were hanging in the closet on her special padded hangers and all her shoes were on the closet floor. And I told Leland about the river. Not the imaginary one but the real one I'd discovered when I came to the end of the mill building on my way to the store. I told him how there was a little dam of rocks and a real waterfall and little frothy places where the water pooled up behind a boulder or a log. How you could throw things in like sticks and paper boats and watch them get carried away, twisting and turning, as if they had some power all their own. He was going to love the river.

Mama wrote about Leland's big audition and how they were still waiting to hear if he'd gotten the part. Seemed she was always waiting to hear about something. Sometimes I'd think how Leland might be all grown up before anyone got around to hiring him, and I'd think how surprised they'd all be, all those directors and movie people, when in walked some big tall man instead of the little boy they expected.

"I thought she was coming east as soon as they got that audition out of the way," Gram told Daddy.

"No point in starting out until they hear the results, Ma. There's just no point in that."

I could tell Daddy was as disappointed as I was that things were still up in the air. He tried to act like it was just the way he'd expected, but I knew it wasn't.

Mama sent new publicity photos of Leland, and he looked real cute. But for some reason Gram didn't think so. She was really mad.

"How long you going to let her pour more and more money down the drain like this?" she asked, shaking one of the photos in Daddy's face. "Just when are you going to demand that she stop all this foolishness and assume her proper place by your side?"

"I agreed to give this a chance, Ma. We've only been separated a couple of months. I have to give Loreen more than a couple of months."

He looked so tired that the skin around his eyes was purple, and his mouth seemed too limp to open up all the way.

"And it's fine and dandy for your own mother and your only daughter to scrimp and save in this decrepit walk-up while your wife plays the lady in her fine house in Beverly Hills. Oh, she says it's for Leland's future. Of course she says that. But we all know whose future she really has in mind."

Daddy sighed. I knew he hated these confrontations with Gram, and they'd been occurring on a daily basis lately. Almost anything could set them off. He had agreed to be patient with Mama. But Gram was demanding that he also be the dutiful only son she'd trained for so many years. Trying to keep such a balance seemed to be wearing him out.

I put one of the pictures of Leland on the little bureau in my room. It was the one where he's tap dancing away while he smiles into the camera and waves a top hat in the air. I thought how it was just amazing that he could do all those things at one time and how I'd bet my bottom dollar most other six-year-olds couldn't come close. At times like that, I'd also think how Mama must be right. Somebody would be bound to see how talented Leland was. The world probably really was just waiting for him to dance across some movie screen and cheer everybody up.

CHAPTER FIVE

By Labor Day, Leland still hadn't heard any-thing, and I was going to have to register for school or risk breaking the law. That's what Gram kept saying, but it wasn't like we were trying to deceive anybody. Daddy just couldn't seem to decide without Mama's help if I should be going to seventh grade at the public school across town or at the parochial school down the street. Just before the first day of classes, Daddy picked Monroe Elementary because it was free.

"Every little bit counts, Mary Francis," he said as though we were saving up for something big. "And you can go to catechism class on Sunday to learn about your faith."

It really didn't matter to me either way. I already knew what I believed. And at either place I'd have to make new friends and learn whole new ways of doing things. I figured my introduction to the eastern seaboard was just about to begin. Everything so far had just been warm-up exercises.

I was glad that he'd picked Monroe, though, when I discovered they had a band that practiced on Thursdays.

To get to the school, I also had to pass LeGrande's and the library twice a day and could cross over and walk along the river for almost the entire mile and a half beyond our mill.

We had started calling it ours to distinguish it from the other mills around. Parts of it were boarded up and dark, but small sections were always busy as beehives with people coming and going for three shifts and bells and buzzers going off when shifts changed. At night, one whole end was lit up like an amusement park, and I told Leland about it because he had always been afraid of the dark. I told him how everything was forever wide awake across the street and how that made it seem like it really wasn't night at all sometimes.

As far as Gram was concerned, the best thing about the mill was the yardage outlet store on one end, where you could get fabric remnants and bolt ends. She discovered it in the middle of the summer, and she was really happy about it. Oh, she still complained when Daddy was home, but she even sang once in a while when I was around and she had something to make on her sewing machine. Sometimes it was potholders, sometimes tea cozies and aprons. By Halloween she had a whole pile of stuff for me to start delivering to LeGrande's on a regular basis. They charged fifteen cents for the potholders, thirty cents for the tea cozies, and sixty cents for each apron. Gram got half and she'd give me what she called a commission. I would have done it for nothing.

"You've got to bloom where you are planted, Mary Francis," she started saying after discovering the motto on a tin of tea. It became her answer to everything, except when she went on one of her tirades against Mama. In fact, as more and more time went on, she began to act as if Mama wouldn't be able to bloom here or anyplace else. I started listening very closely to what she said and the way she said it. I didn't want her to do anything to keep Mama away even longer. The black way she went on and on, it almost seemed like she had it in her power to keep Mama away forever.

The day we learned that Leland was going to have a small part in a real live movie I wasn't sure if Daddy was happy for Mama and Leland or worried that this would make the separation last even longer. The news was definitely something he could use against Gram's long harangues, though. Mama wasn't nearly as misguided as Gram insisted she was. He had the proof.

Gram couldn't help but brag about it to Mrs. Feingold, rushing downstairs as soon as Daddy went to work. She didn't brag about Mama but about having a grandson who was making a movie.

The weather was getting a whole lot colder than we were used to, and Gram stopped making things to sell long enough to sew us each a woolen coat. Mine was dark blue with red, white, and blue buttons and hers was a musty color called dusty rose that didn't look like winter. Daddy took us to a dry-goods store in town for things like woolen hats and mittens, heavy stockings, and galoshes — things we'd never needed in California. Gram said it was beginning to remind her of when she was a girl and so anemic all the time that she could never get really warm.

"Don't go making Mary Francis think we're all gonna freeze to death, Ma. Why, it isn't even Thanksgiving yet," said Daddy. He had a load of coal delivered that next week, though.

The beautiful red and gold leaves that had burned their colors into the air were dropping off the trees in giant drifts. It had been sudden. One day everything was green and beginning to yellow; another and the trees were bursting into flame or all gold and smoldering. Too soon the ground was covered in leaves. By Thanksgiving, Daddy said, all those tree branches would be absolutely bare.

Some sadness in the time of year made me miss Mama even more. I wanted her to come soon so she could help me pick out dress patterns and tell me how I should wear my hair. It was the one thing she seemed to think was just right about me. I'd worn my hair, dark and thick like hers, in braids ever since I could remember. I noticed the very first day of school that nobody in seventh grade wore braids, but when I let my hair hang down loose, it trailed over my back in strands that didn't want to go in the same direction, and I wasn't sure how to curl it up like the other girls did. Elsbeth Murray, a friendly girl who had sat right down at the cafeteria table with me from the start, mentioned how her hair had been long like mine but that she'd cut it the end of that very summer. I didn't let on, but it would be hard for me to make a drastic decision like that without Mama.

"Don't go setting your mind on any particular time for your Mama's arrival, Mary Francis, or you're bound to be disappointed," Gram told me once when Daddy wasn't around. Sometimes I could see that Gram missed Mama a little bit herself. They had been together non-stop before we left. You must get sort of used to someone who is always there like that. And I was sure she missed Leland. You had to miss a good little boy like him.

"You look like some wild thing," said Gram the day I started off to school with my hair loose. "There must be something you can do with that hair!"

Between us, all we could think of was to tie it back with seam-binding tape. My ears had always been un-covered when I wore braids, so it seemed normal at first, but they felt as exposed as two little wind tunnels in this cold snap that didn't seem to have any end.

When I wrote to ask Mama what I should do, she wrote back by airmail that it was time I had a good professional haircut. She said that I should go to the beauty parlor and get my hair styled, how I might look just swell in one of the new bobs or a nice loose permanent wave.

"Of course she'd think of the expensive solution," said Gram when I told her. "If it's a haircut you want, I can do it for you with my sewing shears in two shakes of a lamb's tail."

She sat me down right then and there, and I thought she might be going to play around with my hair a while like Mama did sometimes, trying it different ways. But before I had a chance to consider anything, she combed it out straight and sliced such a regular line that my hair might have been chopped off with a hatchet.

"Always had a good eye," she said, looking closely at what she'd done. "There now." She held up a hand mirror so I could see. "A nice clean trim was all you needed."

My dark wavy hair, which had reached the middle of my back just moments before, now hung down over my ears and tucked under the lobes as if trying to hide. I felt shorn. I felt bare-naked. I looked ten years older.

"Now you look like you might be ready for high school in a few years after all," said Gram. She swept up the cuttings and put a handful to save in my open palm as I held it out in shock. "And it didn't cost us one red penny."

Daddy's favorite saying, "You get what you pay for,"

came instantly to mind. Why had I let her do this? Why did I sit right down like that? What was wrong with me that I could have allowed my grandmother, who knew nothing about style or fashion, to cut off all my hair in one fell swoop? Now Mama would be even more certain to tell people, complete strangers sometimes, how I resemble my father's side of the family and how Leland is an absolute carbon copy of her.

When I begged Daddy to take me someplace to have my head repaired, he laughed and said I looked just fine. Was he blind? Did Gram or Daddy ever really look at me? Did they ever see me at all?

Luckily, with my coat collar pulled up, my beautiful blue hat almost covered my ugly haircut for the trip from home to school. Maybe on the day she bought it, Mama's sixth sense had told her I'd be needing the hat for some emergency like this very one. But after putting my lunch in my locker and getting out the things I'd need, it was clear that I was going to have to take off the hat and face the hundreds of eyes that were arriving minute by minute. The halls were crawling with eyes. I had never seen so many, and they had never been so interested in my hair before. When I saw Elsbeth Murray's eyes heading right for me, I froze. My stomach lurched into my mouth. My knees began to shake.

It was just amazing how I thought of Nora right then. What would she have done? Where would she have gone? It was a miraculous thought, and I suddenly realized without any doubt that if I ever needed her gift, it was right now. Even though I hadn't tried it out since before the family separated, I had to see if it would work in this particular geographic location and special situation. I didn't even have time to think about it, which was probably a good thing. I had to do it right away and that was that. I had to get the wish going and just let go.

The last thing I saw while in my normal state were the faces of Elsbeth Murray, Joanne Connery, and Dolores Fitzpatrick forming a semicircle of surprise and disapproval. They had each been about to say something, I could tell that much, and I was sure I wasn't going to want to hear what it was, so — *whoosh* — I left. Well not really *whoosh* (that would come later) but maybe *puff, puff, puff,* and though it was a little slow going at first, my spirit finally made the big break from my body in as painless and indescribable a way as all those other times. I didn't soar or anything. I mean I didn't go as far as the high windows near the front entrance, I just sort of hovered around, placeless, like I wasn't really filling space at all. And I could see from wherever my spirit was that those girls were still saying what they had to say, but I couldn't hear any of it. It wasn't even important.

Judging from the look on my face, my ears weren't hearing anything either. I was startled, however, when I, when the Mary Francis down on the ground, started to walk off to class with the group. I hadn't known that was possible. And it relieved me a great deal because I wouldn't have wanted her to become some obstacle in everybody's way, and I surely wouldn't have wanted to be marked absent and have the attendance secretary call Gram and worry her or send the truant officer out to our apartment.

Since I'd never done this before in public, so to speak, I wasn't at all sure how or where I could come back. And a strange pull that had almost gone unnoticed before seemed to be growing stronger and stronger as I stayed away. It was such a powerful attraction, so peaceful and welcoming in a warm, spinning kind of way, and it didn't want to let my spirit loose.

Hey, I thought, and the word seemed visible. *I've got to get back.* Who was I talking to? I wasn't sure. God? Unseen spirits? There wasn't any answer.

And it was so hard to wrench myself away. In fact, I had to control my panic and make one attempt after another before I was actually able to lurch slowly back into my body during first period. Mr. Kyper was deep into fractions by that time. When he turned from the board and called my name, I didn't have the right answer, but at least I had one. And though I still felt naked and ugly and somewhat breathless, at least I was sitting down and there were fewer eyes upon me.

By lunchtime, nobody seemed to be staring and

Elsbeth told me how they'd all decided I was very brave to come to school looking so different from everybody else.

"The braids were one thing," she said, "so out of fashion —"

"But this square look does make you seem much more mature," said Dolores. "We've decided we like it." She looked at the others, who were smiling and nodding. "Just forget all the things we said this morning."

How could I forget what I hadn't even heard? And would I ever be brave enough to use this amazing solution to a problem again?

CHAPTER SIX

MAMA HAD WRITTEN THAT LELAND'S MOVIE WAS A low-budget film called *Dancing Feet,* and I started looking for it in the local papers and in the *Boston Post* that Daddy bought on Sundays. When Gram saw me turning the pages she said, "Don't go wasting your time looking for that movie, Mary Francis. If it ever really gets made, which I doubt, they won't release it until next year or maybe even a year or two after that."

"How do you know?"

"Haven't you ever noticed any of that stuff they put in coming attractions? They always say things like, 'to be released in the spring.' Things like that."

"But you're talking about years. Mama called it a low-budget quick little production. It's not going to take years."

"I just don't want you disappointed is all."

Lately it seemed Gram was always trying to save me from disappointment. She didn't want me disappointed if Mama didn't show up when I expected. She didn't want me disappointed if my hair grew back as slowly as hers did. Maybe what she really wanted was that I stop hoping for things. If I did hope for too much, wouldn't some of it be more apt to come true if there were a little extra?

A major disappointment for me, and one that Gram hadn't known to warn me about, had been when I brought my accordion to school on the day for band tryouts only to find that it wasn't considered a regulation band instrument.

"We could use a piano player," Mr. Gupper, the bandleader, had said as though all I had to do was sit down at the piano and start playing.

"I don't play the piano, Mr. Gupper," I told him. "The accordion is a very different instrument."

He'd looked surprised at that, and when I said that I wasn't one bit interested in learning the violin, he seemed a little angry.

"Just take that . . . that big music box on home now and come back when you've learned one of the more conventional instruments that might be an addition to our little band. I expect the accordion goes over big in Beverly Hills, California, but it's no use here."

He was wrong about that. I hadn't performed anywhere in Beverly Hills after Mama had decided the roller skating idea was such a bad one.

Since I didn't have another interesting thing to talk about, I started mentioning to the kids at school about how my brother was in the movies. At first they didn't believe me, but after I brought in the picture of him dancing, most of them changed their minds. For a little while it was as if I was a celebrity even though I was just his sister. And I guess they thought his talent must have rubbed off on me in some way, because Elsbeth and Dolores started saying how I should be in the holiday talent show.

That really got me thinking about the roller skating idea again. Maybe it would work better now without my braids whipping around. There was a roller rink in town. Maybe I could rent real shoe-boot skates and practice my skating there. And there was a big stage in the auditorium at school with a nice flat wooden floor and an orchestra pit that would keep me from rolling out into the audience. If I landed on Mr. Gupper, well, so what!

I finally hinted to the kids who kept asking that I was planning on doing something, but I didn't say what it would be. I also started saving my commissions from Gram so I could go to Rollo's Roller Rink on Saturdays. I knew I couldn't practice there with my accordion, but if my legs got good and strong and I learned how to stick one out and glide and how to stop on a dime, then everything would work out fine.

"I hope you aren't going to a place like that to meet friends on the sly," said Gram when I first told her where I was off to. "The kind of friends you meet on the sly are always bad news."

What had made her think such a thing? What did she mean by "a place like that"?

Remembering how the act had been her idea in the first place, I thought that maybe I should let her in on my secret. But the way she was so negative about everything lately, I decided not to.

"It's good exercise, Gram," I said. "I'm just going there for the exercise. It's too cold outside to do much of anything that's fun."

She had to agree with me. She'd begun complaining about the cold in October. "Chilblains" was what she started having in November, even though she only left the apartment to go to the remnant outlet.

"Be back before dark," she said, "Your mama's giving us a long-distance call at six o'clock, soon after Forest gets in the door."

Daddy worked on some Saturdays, and this was one of them. Mama had written a week before to tell us she'd be making this long-distance call. It was another extravagance Gram didn't approve of, but it took her interest like something forbidden and exotic, and you could tell she'd been waiting for the call ever since reading Mama's letter.

"I wonder if she has important news." I said.

"There's scant chance of that. No, I wouldn't be planning on anything like that."

I wasn't planning on anything but the sound of Mama's voice. She'd called once before, but the connection had been bad and Daddy was so afraid of talking too long that he'd put the receiver down when three minutes were up exactly. It was before I'd even had a chance to say hello. I'd cried myself to sleep that night.

He had apologized in the morning and said how he just wasn't thinking and that it would be different next time. Knowing there might be a next time made it easier to bear. I wrote Mama and said, "Don't you let Daddy hang up like that and don't you hang up again until I've had my chance." I didn't even get to talk to Leland and find out how he liked going to Hollywood Professional School on a bus. He seemed so little to be doing something like that. I wondered if he was afraid.

I walked really fast to Rollo's Roller Rink. It was twice as far as school and my feet felt twice as shivery when I got there. The tips of my fingers ached and my nose was red. Daddy'd been telling me for weeks not to complain because it really wasn't even winter yet, so I figured the cold that was coming must be too painful for words. Inside Rollo's it wasn't much warmer. There was a strong smell of raw wood coming from the walls and railings. They were unfinished and full of gaping knotholes. And there was a steady roaring sound that filled me up so I couldn't think. For a while I just stood there and let it wash through me like thunder. And then I realized it was coming from all those rolling wooden wheels going round and round and round.

Only a few people had on skates you had to fasten with a key. It was thrilling to notice that and to think how lucky I was to have been born at a time in history when there were shoe-boot roller skates.

The skates I rented weren't such a good fit, but the very idea that I could lace them up my ankles made me content to have my feet rock around a little inside. Soon I was pushing off and rolling around with everybody else. It got easier and easier with each lap, and my ankles didn't wobble at all. I even started trying crossovers after watching other skaters do it. Elsbeth and Dolores were skating together with their arms crossed in front of them and holding hands, doing what people around here called the shottish. When they waved at me, they lost count and almost fell down. I wondered, was this what Gram meant by meeting kids on the sly?

It had started getting dark real early, so when the big clock in the center of the rink said four, I glided over to the edge and took my skates back to the rental desk. I waved at Elsbeth and Dolores as if the three of us had been skating around together all afternoon.

As soon as I got in the door of the apartment, Gram said to set the table so we could eat right on the dot of 5:30 or whenever Daddy got home. It made me think that maybe one of us would still be chewing something when Mama called or that I might start to choke on a mouthful right when the phone started ringing and not be able to say a word.

"Why can't we eat right after she calls?" I asked. It seemed like a perfectly reasonable request.

"And there's the best part of the evening gone, just like that," said Gram. "I surely don't want to miss *Gang Busters* again. There's no reason in the world we can't get through a meal in one half-hour. No reason at all."

It didn't make sense, but I knew nothing I said was going to change her mind. Her pot roast would be done to perfection and juiceless at 5:30. Not a minute before or after. The turnips would be soft and sticky as glue, just the way she liked them.

But that didn't mean I could eat anything. When Daddy came home and Gram all but carried him to a chair, I felt like I couldn't breathe let alone take a bite of food.

"Mary Francis, you'll be too weak to hold up your end of the conversation if you don't put something in your stomach," said Gram.

"Leave her alone, Ma," Daddy said. "She's too excited to eat. I haven't much appetite myself, truth to tell." He squeezed his baked potato and just let it sit there.

"Well, I never!" said Gram. "You'd think Loreen was the Queen of the May. You'd think she was some great big movie star herself." She dug into the food on her own plate as if there was no tomorrow. "Go ahead, the two of you," she said between bites. "Sit there mooning while my good dinner gets cold. But don't expect me to go warming anything up again. There's nothing worse than warmed-over pot roast."

If that meant she wasn't going to want to talk to Mama, there was going to be more time for me. I didn't want to get Gram any angrier, so I stayed put. But I couldn't see the clock from the kitchen table, so every little while I'd ask Daddy what time it was on his watch.

"It's three minutes later than the last time you asked," he said each time. He'd begun to pick absently at his own food. It didn't look as though he even knew what he was eating.

Close to 6:00, he put his fork down, folded his napkin, and began staring at the telephone on its own little table. Gram had finished what was on her plate and rushed to clear the kitchen table.

At 6:00, Daddy looked at his watch, crossed one wrist over the other, and held his own hands. At five past, he took off his watch and gave it a shake. At ten past he put it back on.

"Do you think we have the time right?" I asked at last. "Is it the right day?"

Gram took out the letter, put on her reading glasses, and read out loud. "'Leland and I will be putting through a call to all of you by long-distance on Saturday night at 6:00 P.M. your time.' Can't be any clearer than that!" She handed me the letter so I could read it, too.

"Maybe her phone's out of order," I said. Sometimes

60

the phones in an entire Beverly Hills neighborhood would be what Gram called "on the fritz."

"Could be," said Daddy. "Could just be."

"Maybe the other party won't give it up," I said. We had a two-party line in California.

"The other party is Mrs. Moran," said Gram. "She goes to bed in the middle of the afternoon. Even accounting for time zones, she'd be sound asleep."

Daddy got up and took his plate to the sink.

I got up and checked the clock on the desk. It was 6:15.

"Maybe she meant six-thirty," I said.

"Maybe, Mary Francis."

"Maybe you should try calling her. That's a good idea, isn't it?"

"No," he said, surprising me again. "It isn't a good idea. Tomorrow maybe. Another day. But not now."

"Just think," said Gram. She was speaking in such a quiet way for her. "Now you won't have to miss your favorite programs."

"Maybe she's sick," I said. "Maybe Leland's sick."

"I don't think so, honey," said Daddy. He hardly ever called me that. "I think we probably don't have to worry about them. Maybe something came up. Maybe she forgot."

I can play that game, too, I thought.

"Yeah, that's probably it. Something came up."

CHAPTER SEVEN

I THOUGHT MAMA WOULD SURELY CALL ON SUNDAY because she knew Daddy would be home and the long distance charges were cheaper. I still wondered why Daddy wasn't calling her, why he wasn't worried. Maybe there'd been an earthquake that nobody here knew about yet. Maybe she or Leland had been run over in traffic. Maybe the house had burned down. I couldn't concentrate on my homework or anything else, I was so worried. Why were Gram and Daddy acting unconcerned and poking around the apartment the way they always did?

On Monday, right after I'd come in the door from school and while Gram was sewing up a storm on her machine, the phone rang. When Gram didn't stop, I knew she hadn't heard it, and I picked up the receiver, yelling over the noise.

It was Mama. I had to stretch the telephone's long cord into the kitchen so I could hear her. Even then it was hard because she seemed to be whispering.

"Mama," I yelled, and she immediately told me to

hush. She said, "Talk softly, Mary Francis, so your grandmother doesn't hear. Did she hear the phone? Does she know it's me?"

"She's sewing, Mama. It only rang once before I picked it up."

"Good. That's good. Real lucky."

"You didn't call Saturday night, Mama. We all waited, but you didn't call." I didn't say it like a question. I wanted her to feel real bad about it.

"I couldn't, honey." She paused. She didn't give a single reason. "You've got to listen to me very carefully now."

"I'm listening, Mama."

"Your daddy wrote me a nasty letter, you see. It was just so unlike him, I feel sure Gram was behind it. Did they mention anything to you?"

"No, Mama. They didn't say a thing."

"Good. That's good. Well . . . the gist of it was that Daddy says he can't keep making payments on this house and pay the rent for that apartment, too. That he can't keep supporting two households — it's just too much of a strain."

"It's probably true, Mama." I didn't see what was so nasty about that.

"And, would you believe it, Mary Francis, he wants Leland and me to pack right up and move east. Or else."

"Or else what?"

"He didn't say exactly. But I didn't like what the phrase implied."

"What do you want me to do?"

"Oh, honey. I don't know. I don't know what any of us can do. But I did have a thought."

I was beginning to remember about these thoughts of hers and how they could wreak havoc with my life, but I listened.

"I thought that if you could persuade Daddy to send us tickets on the Union Pacific for Christmas, we could all spend the holiday together. And, of course, he and I would have a chance to discuss everything in a more civilized manner."

"You mean you wouldn't be moving here for good? You and Leland would just be visiting?"

"Don't put it like that, Mary Francis. It would be more like a first step to our reconciliation. Yes. That's what it would be."

Was it true? Did she mean it this time? I had wanted to hear the sound of her voice so badly I'd dreamed about it. But what was she saying? Was she trying to trick Daddy and did she want me to help her do it?

"You'll help me won't you, honey? You'll talk to Daddy? He always listens to you. Do it some time when Gram is out someplace else. Yes, that's the best idea. Pick the time very carefully, sweetie. Tell him Leland misses him so much."

"Does he miss me?"

"Why, of course, Mary Francis. He misses you almost as much as I do."

That wasn't enough. Not nearly enough.

"So, you see, honey, I couldn't call on Saturday right after that awful letter. Why, I was just so taken aback!"

"Don't you want to know how I am or anything?"

"Of course I do, sweetheart. But you sound just fine. And I really have to go now. You know how it is. We'll catch up at Christmas." She blew little kisses into the phone before she said good-bye.

I didn't have the faintest idea how it was. With Mama, I never did. All the things I'd been saving up to tell her, like about school and the weather here, and she hadn't given me a single chance. She hadn't even told me anything about Leland or put him on the phone. But she wanted to come at Christmas. She definitely wanted to do that, and that was better news than if she didn't want to come at all.

I waited for days before bringing it up, paying close attention to what she'd said about choosing the time carefully.

Daddy and I were on our way to the big market on the main road that had so much more than the little ones in the neighborhoods. It was comfortable going places in the car with Daddy. He didn't talk much, but he didn't expect me to say much either. We talked or didn't just as we pleased.

I knew it was the kind of opportune time Mama had hinted at, but I hated to spoil things by bringing up Mama's plan and making him go real quiet and distant. And I didn't want him to think I didn't sympathize with his predicament or that I was all on Mama's side no matter what. I tried to be on Mama's side. I wanted it to be a good side, something that would make all these changes in our lives worthwhile. And I really wanted her and Leland to come for Christmas. But I didn't see why Daddy should have to spend all that extra money for train fare if they weren't even planning to stay.

It wasn't until we were actually in the market that I was able to bring up Christmas. Turkeys were on sale for Thanksgiving, and I thought out loud how it might be nice to have a turkey for Christmas, too, and wouldn't it be swell if we could buy one then that was big enough for all of us? Maybe twenty pounds?

"Doesn't look as if we're going to be needing a turkey that big," said Daddy. "Maybe next year."

He asked the grocer for a small bird and ten pounds of potatoes.

"There's a train from L.A. to Boston isn't there?" I asked. I felt sneaky pretending not to know.

"Of course there's a train." He turned to the grocer and asked him to weigh out some green beans.

"Why couldn't Mama and Leland come for a visit on the train?"

"You'd settle for a visit now? Well, if that doesn't take the cake!"

He picked up a squash and thumped it so hard the grocer lifted it right out of his hands.

"Sorry, Mr. Livermore," Daddy told him.

"I just meant," I continued, "I mean . . . we could see them for a little while that way. They might like it here. They might decide to stay."

Daddy had stopped ordering things and Mr. Livermore was looking annoyed. He moved to the next customer.

"You're talking as if Leland has a say in all of this," said Daddy. "He's just a little boy. He does whatever his mama wants him to. You know that."

"I know it, Daddy."

His voice turned quiet.

"And, Mary Francis, let's be honest here. Can you see your mama falling in love with this place and wanting to stay?"

"No, Daddy. But I'd like to think she might fall in love with us again. It's crazy I guess. I guess you're right."

"I wish I could believe she would." He said this so quietly I almost didn't hear him.

I picked up an apple under a sign that said these

were the last of the Macintoshes. I was looking it over just as Mr. Livermore took it from me and put it in a paper sack. He asked how many we wanted and Daddy said two pounds, "and three or four of those Florida grapefruit."

"You know what I think the trouble is?" I asked, looking Daddy right in the eyes. "I think the trouble is she just believes too hard in things."

"In the wrong things."

"But she doesn't know they're the wrong things. She thinks they're beautiful things — and dreams about to come true."

Daddy sort of chuckled under his breath.

Mr. Livermore was now standing right in front of us and tapping his stubby fingers on the counter.

"Two cans of tomatoes, Mr. Livermore. And five pounds of flour." Daddy looked down at me when Mr. Livermore turned around.

"You know, I think you might be just a little bit right about that. Just a little."

"You know how I know?" I asked. I pointed to a jar of honey and Mr. Livermore put it with our order. "Because I have a tendency to believe in the wrong things, too."

"That's just because she's filled you up with crazy notions."

"There's a sale on Hershey's chocolate," said Mr. Livermore. Dad took a package and a bunch of carrots.

"Or maybe because I have a few crazy notions of my own," I said.

"You're a smart girl, Mary Francis. I wish your mama was as smart as you."

It seemed like a very disloyal thing for him to be saying and for me to be hearing.

If only I'd been smart enough to get him interested in the Christmas plan. He seemed to have forgotten about that. I couldn't let him.

He checked his list from Gram, and Mr. Livermore went to get a box of confectioners' sugar, a package of prunes, and a bag of puffed wheat.

"Maybe the Christmas trip could be everybody's present — except Gram's," I said. "I wouldn't want anything else. If Leland and Mama could come just for a little while, I wouldn't ask for one other thing."

"I don't know, Mary Francis. It's not about not wanting them to come. It's about this whole crazy idea of hers. It's about trying to pay for things when you haven't the money. And there's one other thing." He looked down at the floor and away from Mr. Livermore, who was still gathering up our order. At first I thought Daddy had dropped something.

"What's that, Daddy?"

"Wait till we get outside," he whispered. He paid Mr. Livermore and put all the things that were now on the counter into the oilcloth bags with handles that Gram had made for this very purpose.

Back on the sidewalk, he said, "It's like . . ." He couldn't seem to finish so he started again. "It's just that she doesn't seem to know who's boss. I mean, I want to take care of her and Leland, but she isn't really letting me do it in the only way I know how."

"You *are* the boss, Daddy."

"No, Mary Francis. You know I'm not. And Loreen does, too. But couldn't she just pretend a little bit? Couldn't she sometimes act as if what I think is important to her? As if *I'm* important to her?"

I'd been making excuses for Mama for a long time for not thinking I was important, but it was a surprise to find out that Daddy was feeling the exact same way. It wasn't a good way to feel, and I didn't want there to be two of us in this terrible predicament. Maybe what he needed was to pretend more, too.

"I've been pretending for years," he said when we were back in the car.

I couldn't think of anything to say after that. It wasn't going to be as nice a ride as the one coming here, but I'd said what I had to. And I guess Daddy had said what he had to, too. I was glad that he'd told me I was smart. And it was good that he trusted me enough to tell me how he felt. But I wished all of a sudden that he hadn't.

CHAPTER EIGHT

I DECIDED THAT IF THINGS WORKED OUT SO MAMA and Leland could actually come for Christmas, it would be a sign that my talent show performance was going to be a showstopper. Oh, I didn't care anymore if Mama thought I was good enough to put in the movies, but I did want her to be proud of me for once. I guess that was what I had really wanted all along. And I desperately wanted her and Leland to see my premiere.

Since I was sure we couldn't afford accordion lessons and I didn't know where on earth to find another teacher anyway, it looked like I'd have to practice on my own. I had plenty of sheet music from the last series of lessons, and there were lots of exercises that I could still remember. I mean, all the roller skating in the world wasn't going to impress anyone if I couldn't play the accordion like there was no tomorrow once I got up on that stage.

The trouble was, any time I picked to practice, Gram would either find a job for me to do all of a sudden or she'd start whipping up something on her machine so I couldn't hear the notes. I guess the idea was that she

71

didn't want to hear the notes either. What she couldn't have understood was that I wouldn't be able to play anything worth listening to by Christmas if I didn't get to work on it.

After many episodes like this, I learned to take advantage of her trips to the mill outlet. Luckily, they were pretty frequent. In fact, there was a pile of remnants at one end of the living room that was almost as tall as I was. Mama would hate looking at that.

It was a big mistake to mention the fact to Gram, though.

"It doesn't matter what your mama thinks about this living room," she said. "She isn't living in it."

I had to admit that I didn't miss the law and order that had prevailed in our other living room. Mama had picked what she called a "restful" color scheme and everything had its own perfect place. She would say how her décor couldn't be disturbed, how it contributed to her tranquillity. Leland and I spent a lot of time out-of-doors, which she said was the only proper place for our brand of roughhousing. She also said how that was what living in California was all about.

I wondered what she'd think of all the time we had to spend in the house now because of the weather. When I mentioned that to Gram, she said, "As if we actually had a house, a decent house, as if we weren't being forced to live like vagrants because of your mother's excesses. None of us would have a reason to complain about being indoors during the cold months, if we had a decent house."

Another time she asked me did I know how lucky we were that Daddy had a good job during "these terrible times" when most people were finding it hard to land any job at all and to keep up one "living establishment," let alone two. She said how this "peculiar domestic situation" of ours couldn't go on for much longer, that something was going to give and she hoped it wouldn't be her Forest.

It was the first time I ever remember seeing Gram start to cry. She didn't go all the way but just sniffled and dabbed at her eyes. It happened to be the very same day that Daddy came home all smiles, saying how he'd wired money for the train tickets to Mama just hours earlier.

Gram didn't say a word. She just picked up the dress she was mending, went to her room, and shut the door.

Daddy watched her go, but his mood didn't change one bit. He gave me a big hug and said, "Now maybe things will get back to normal around here, Mary Francis." I tried to imagine what he could mean, because I didn't think for a minute that it was going to feel anything like normal once Mama arrived. Sometimes I didn't even remember clearly what it had been like. Of course she would be sleeping in his bed again and that would seem more like the way it should be. I suspected he'd been real lonesome and would be glad of that.

I hoped he wasn't expecting too much from this reunion, although I wasn't about to spoil the anticipation by saying so. I'd noticed that looking forward to things was sometimes better than the way they turned out to be when you actually got right up next to them. It seemed I was destined to prove that fact to myself over and over again.

It was a school day when the train with Mama and Leland on it came into Boston. Daddy was inclined to let me go with him to pick them up, but Gram said it was a bad idea to take a day off from school with Christmas vacation and all those idle days on the horizon.

Gram and I worked like a house afire to shine everything up as much as possible. I knew exactly why I wanted Mama to be impressed, but I couldn't imagine why Gram was so concerned about it unless it was to prove that we could get along just fine all by ourselves.

Still, I wasn't surprised when Mama walked in the door and kind of crumbled. It was just for an instant and you could tell she was trying to keep up a good front. She held out her arms to me, and I folded up inside them. She smelled exactly like I remembered, like some kind of flower too delicate to be real. Leland started pulling on my skirt and jumping around like a puppy let off its leash.

I showed him the bunk beds right away and took him down to the river. On our way back, the Murphy twins asked us to play marbles, but Leland didn't know how and was too shy. When we came into the apartment, the grownups were sitting around the kitchen table and drinking coffee just the way I'd seen them do a million times before. Mama was telling about Leland's school and his auditions and Gram was showing Mama her potholders. Dad was just sitting there looking happy and satisfied and holding Mama's hand. It seemed perfect, just the way I'd hoped against hope that it would be. It *was* perfect.

Then Mama looked at me and asked, "Why is your accordion sitting right out there in the middle of everything, Mary Francis? And what is that unsightly mountain of scraps doing at one end of the living room? Isn't there a ragman in this town to pick up refuse like that?"

Three questions. Three short questions and suddenly everything was completely different. I was hurrying back to my room with my bulky instrument wheezing and thumping. Gram was shouting at Mama. Daddy was running his hand through the hair he still had and saying, "Oh, for Pete's sake!" Leland had started to cry.

I went back and picked him up, which wasn't easy anymore since he'd grown so much, and I took him to what was our room for a while. I started reading him one of my Buck Rogers comic books and after just a few pages he stopped crying. By the end of the second comic, he was fast asleep sitting up.

When I found I couldn't lift him onto the top bunk, I left him on the bottom one and climbed up on top myself. I lay there wide awake for a long time and watched whatever I could see out the window. A flock of little birds flew by looking like a burst of dark leaves against the cold sky. I could hear angry voices rise and fall in the other room, sometimes Mama's, sometimes Gram's, once Daddy's. What they were saying wasn't clear and I didn't try to sort it out.

Just before I fell asleep myself, I realized that this was how it used to be all the time, that this was what I'd been wishing for.

In the morning, Leland was still in bed, playing with the two little cars he'd brought with him. I dressed for school in the bathroom. Daddy's room was shut tight, and he was in the kitchen tying his tie and putting on his shoes and socks. He said that we should be real quiet because Mama was sleeping in. Gram was cooking bacon and eggs in the big iron skillet.

"I'm not cooking two breakfasts," she said to him. She pulled open the doors of the toaster and put a slice of bread in each side.

"No one's asking you to do that," said Daddy. "Loreen will help herself. Don't go making problems, Ma, where there are none."

"Lord knows I don't have to make up problems around here."

She slid an over-easy egg onto my plate. It was just the way I liked it, and I pierced it with my fork to make the yolk run out.

"Should I get Leland?"

"I'll get him," said Gram. She called down the hall as if he were down the block somewhere.

"Ma, I asked you to be quiet! Would it be such a hardship for you to keep your voice down?"

"You never use that tone with me when she's not around."

"And you go out of your way to be aggravating when she is."

Leland came down the hall on his knees, pushing his cars ahead of him and pretending to rev the engines.

"Breakfast is served, young man," said Gram. "From the looks of you, you could use a big hearty meal."

"Now what is that all about?" asked Daddy.

"Just look at the boy, Forest. He's all skin and bones. He probably hasn't had a real breakfast or a balanced meal since we left. It breaks my heart."

"You don't know that, Ma. There's no way you can know that. He's a growing boy."

He gave Leland a soft punch in the belly.

"Isn't that right, son?"

Leland flinched. He crossed his arms around himself protectively.

11

"I like puffed wheat," he said. "With sugar on it."

I quickly poured him a bowl before Gram could insist that he eat bacon and eggs, which we both knew he hated.

"Thanks, Mary Francis," he said in the small sweet voice I had missed so much.

He turned up his nose at the canned orange juice we'd been drinking since we moved back east. He was right. It didn't taste anything like real oranges.

When I left for school, Leland was playing on the floor again, Mama was still asleep, and Gram had turned on the radio to hear her morning prayer program.

Dad had gone to work whistling. I thought how strange that was, unless, of course, all the wrangling of the night before had led to some solution to our problem that I wasn't aware of.

All day I thought about the three of them together in that apartment, about Mama and Gram together in such close quarters. I wondered sometimes if it would ever be like the story about the gingham dog and the calico cat in one of Leland's books where the wrangling got so fierce, they ate each other up.

Maybe when I had more time to practice and got real good at separating myself from my body, I could teach it to Gram and she wouldn't even be able to hear Mama. But then I remembered how Nora had said it was a gift. How it was my gift. How it wasn't the kind you could give away even if you wanted to.

As soon as I came in the door from school that day, Mama clutched my elbow and said that she needed to get out of the house. She said she was feeling so cooped up she was fit to be tied.

"Let's walk to that little variety store you told me about, Mary Francis. Just you and me." Gram was at her sewing machine as usual. Leland was coloring at the kitchen table. "I've just gotta stretch my legs."

She took the coat she'd worn coming here, the one she wore winters in Beverly Hills, down from a hook in the front closet. I knew it wasn't going to keep her warm once we got outside, but she hadn't brought anything else. Since she'd grown up in a cold climate, I wondered why she didn't know any better.

When we started down the stairs, she looked at my coat and wrinkled up her nose.

"Where in the world did you get that? Don't tell me—Gram ran it up on the machine! I should have guessed."

"You don't like it, Mama?"

"It hasn't any style, Mary Francis. It's so boxy, and it's at least a whole size too big."

"Gram wanted it to fit for a couple of years."

"It will. It definitely will do that."

"It's really warm."

"Well, I'm glad, honey. I guess that's the important thing."

She picked up some strands of my hair.

"And I suppose she did this, too. I should have known she wouldn't take you to the beauty parlor like I wanted."

"It's okay, Mama. I've gotten used to it."

"We'll fix it up, honey. Don't let me forget."

We were out on the sidewalk by now, and she was taking in great big breaths of cold air.

"I thought I'd go stir crazy for a minute in there. Gram just keeps sewing away. She hasn't been in any mood to talk all day, at least not to me. She and Leland will probably get along just swell now that I'm out of there."

Mama had on her high heels, and I wondered if she knew how far it was to LeGrande's, but I didn't say anything. Maybe she hadn't brought any other shoes.

We had walked about a block when she looked over at the mill and said, "I can't believe you have nothing to look at but that big old ugly building. I mean, couldn't Forest have found an apartment with a decent view at least? It wouldn't be so bad being cooped up in a dreary apartment like that if you had something decent to look at. You know what I mean?"

Once I had known what she meant, but the mill building didn't look ugly to me at all anymore. The way it was always there. The way parts of it were lit up at night. I'd grown accustomed to it. I'd come to count on it.

"Wait'll you see the river, Mama."

I ran ahead. When I got to the end of the next block I turned and called to her.

"Look, Mama! Just look!"

The river was rushing out from behind the mill with such force that the air was filled with spray. In the afternoon light, there were tiny rainbows everywhere.

"Isn't it something?"

She started smiling then and standing still. She clasped her hands in front of her and stared at the river like it was the Pacific Ocean.

"It's beautiful, Mary Francis. What a shame it gets all covered up like that."

"It's all right, Mama. You just have to walk down here, and there it is. It's always there. You can even climb down onto the rocks like it was a beach or something."

"Oh, be careful, honey. You've got to be real careful. Why, look at that strong current! It's not someplace you should go all by yourself. Promise me you won't go down there alone. I'm going to worry now if you don't make me that promise."

I wondered if she could guess how many times I'd already been down there by myself. I was careful. Daddy hadn't worried about it. I wondered if I had to mind her when she wasn't here. After all, there hadn't been a problem when she didn't know anything about it.

She shivered and started hitting her bare hands against her sides to keep them warm. When I didn't say anything, she seemed to forget about the promise.

"I had no idea it would be so cold here. Why, I've been in California for so long, you might say I'm almost native born. I've just put snow and ice and all that right out of my mind."

"Maybe we should go back home and get a sweater to put under your coat," I said. Kids with thin coats at school sometimes wore sweaters underneath.

"And give Gram something else to chide me about? No thank you. Let's just get going. I'll be warm in no time if we keep moving."

By the time we got to LeGrande's, the blue of her lips was coming through her red lip rouge and making her mouth look purple. She rubbed her hands together in front of the potbelly stove and moaned as the blood came back into them.

She bought us mugs of hot cider and some dough-nuts, and we sat in chairs right by the stove. By then the pain had left her face and she was like a little girl discovering a lost doll. She was almost flirty with Mr. LeGrande. Mrs. LeGrande had turned as silent as a bag of flour.

"Isn't this just the most inviting place to be in all the world? And it's just such a Christmasy thing to do. We should have brought Leland. I feel like we're in some kind of Christmas play."

I was glad we hadn't brought Leland so I could have her all to myself like this. Even though she kept looking around like a starry-eyed child and didn't even glance in my direction, I knew I was on her mind. I was near as I could be to her, and I was on her mind. But every time another customer came and the door burst open, a bell would jingle and a shaft of cold air would shoot across our necks. We moved our chairs to one side, but it didn't do any good. As soon as she'd finished her cider she stood up.

"Anything you think we should bring back for Gram?" she asked. "Thread maybe? Some hard candy?"

"She might like the candy, Mama." *And even if she doesn't,* I thought, *Leland and I will appreciate it.*

She bought a fancy jar of hard candy with a golden bow, a couple of marshmallow ice cream cone candies for Leland, and a real maple sugar doll for me. I had wanted one since I first saw them in the glass case. Mama knew it without my telling her. She was good about things like that, about knowing just what would appeal to me. I wondered why she wasn't so good at figuring out the important things.

Walking back, we didn't stop at all but kept moving as fast as we could short of running. It was a little hard to keep up a conversation, but it seemed like a good time to tell her about the talent show that was going to happen right before Christmas vacation. I wanted her to have something to look forward to.

"You mean," she began — she was chewing on one of the licorice whips she'd bought for herself and her breath was coming out in chalky little puffs —"you mean you expect to play your accordion in front of a great big group like that when you haven't had a lesson since you left Beverly Hills?"

"I haven't forgotten anything."

"But, really, Mary Francis. I mean, you have to know your music by heart before you perform it for a great big group like that. The audience will expect you to know your music backwards and forwards."

"I've been practicing, Mama. You'd be surprised at how good I sound. Remember the Tarantella? And the piece about the swan?"

"Hmmm," she said. She didn't stop walking or slow down. "I remember you had a little trouble with the Tarantella at my ladies' club luncheon that Valentine's Day. Why, you forgot one whole page."

"But I know the music now, Mama. I think you'll be proud of me."

I was glad I hadn't told her about the roller skates. I was really glad I'd held that back.

CHAPTER NINE

WE COULD HEAR THE MUSIC AND TAPPING AS SOON AS we'd opened the storm door. Mrs. Feingold had her apartment door open and was leaning way out. She mumbled something and shut it as soon as Mama and I appeared on the stairs.

"Afternoon, Mrs. Feingold," said Mama, real sweet.

Mrs. Krakas was leaning over the railing at the top and looking down at us. She didn't say hello and she didn't budge.

"I just can't get used to the lack of privacy," Mama said loud enough for almost anyone to hear.

We knew the sounds were coming from our apartment, but we didn't know until we got inside that Gram and Leland had rolled up the rug and put a record on the Victrola. When we came in, he threw one of Gram's old summer hats into the air, did a twirling jump, and kept on dancing away to beat the band. He called out, "Look at me, Mary Francis!" without missing a beat. Gram was clapping her hands in time to the music and hooting as if she were at some hoedown. She smiled right out of her eyes. When it came to the end of the record, Leland did a little bow and ran over to Mama.

She clapped as hard as she could and I did, too.

"See what I've been telling you, Ma? Isn't he something! Isn't he something else?"

Gram collapsed into the rocker by the window. She put her hand to her heart like it might leap out the front of her calico dress.

"I have to admit it, Loreen. He's a regular shrunk-down combination of Bo Jangles and that Fred Astaire."

"I told you."

Leland kept tapping even without the music.

"All that talent in one little boy! It's just too much."

"And he can act, too. You should just hear him at those auditions. When he does the *Little Lord Fauntleroy* piece, he all but has those grown-up directors in tears."

"Then why doesn't he get the parts?" I asked. I really wondered. I thought he was terrific, too, and it didn't seem to make any sense.

"I don't understand it myself," said Mama. "It's a complete mystery to me. I take him here and there and everywhere, and we come home empty-handed. I mean, they put us off. They say they'll let us know, that they'll be in touch — things like that. Of course, he did have that one little part. It might just be a steppingstone to something big."

"You never can tell," said Gram.

Gram was surprising me. She was acting almost as caught up in this movie star stuff as Mama.

"He's head and shoulders better than Shirley Temple," said Gram.

Mama seemed mystified.

"Why, I think so, too," she said.

"But you can't sacrifice everybody else in a family for one person's ambitions," said Gram. She brought up this enormous weary sigh as if she'd been saving it. It was like she was warring with herself, like she was casting off some spell. "It just isn't right."

"Even if everyone else would benefit?"

"That's unlikely. With the family spread apart the way it is and the expense of it all. You've got to start thinking of the rest of us, Loreen."

Mama looked like she'd been told she couldn't go to the party no matter how well she behaved. I felt real sorry for her.

For a little while there it had seemed as if Gram and Mama were on the exact same side. Leland must have felt it, too, because he started asking when we were all going to be moving back to Beverly Hills.

As soon as Daddy came home Leland climbed all over him and clung to him like ivy. Daddy had to shake him free to take off his coat.

"Just a minute there, young fella."

"Wanna watch me dance, Daddy?"

"Sure I do, son. Sure I do."

"Wanna come outside and see how fast I can run?"

"You were always a fast runner, Leland." Daddy

chucked him under the chin. "I'll bet you can go like the wind."

"Faster, Daddy. Like lightning."

Mama started easing Leland away.

"Let your daddy unwind a little, Leland. He's only just come in the door."

Those were the exact words she used to say to me, and she was saying them in the exact same way.

"My Lord!" said Gram so loudly we all jumped. "I forgot all about our supper. All that dancing and singing and carrying on, and I forgot to put the meat loaf in the oven."

"That's all right, Ma," said Daddy. "It'll be an excuse to visit that new chicken-and-biscuit place a couple miles outside of town."

"Oh, I do love a good fried chicken," said Mama.

"I always bake my chicken," said Gram. "Always have and always will."

"And it's very delicious, too," said Mama.

It was making me nervous, the way Mama was tight-rope walking around Gram. I wondered how long she could keep it up.

"On the way we can see the big decorated Christmas tree on the green. Wouldn't you like that, Leland?" Daddy picked him up. "There won't be lights all over town like you have in Beverly Hills, but there are a few nice displays here and there."

"It'll be wonderful, sweetheart," Mama told Daddy. She ruffled the fringe of his hair and he beamed all over. "Put your coat back on, Mary Francis." She turned to Gram. "I was just telling Mary Francis how much I admire her new coat. When she told me that you'd made it, Ma, well, I could hardly believe it. You'll be opening up your own tailoring establishment next."

"Not if I can help it," said Gram.

"It was just an expression, Ma. You know what I mean."

"Should I change my dress?" Gram asked Daddy.

"You look just fine, Ma. Put on *your* new coat and show *that* to Loreen."

Gram suddenly became shy, but there was a moment when you could just see her deciding that she was going to have to wear the coat or stay home.

"What a gorgeous shade of pink!" squealed Mama. "Why, it does such nice things for your skin."

"Perks up my wrinkles, does it?"

Mama started to sulk. "Seems I can't say a single thing that you aren't bound and determined to take the wrong way."

"Now, Loreen," said Daddy.

"Oh, I know exactly which way to take things," said Gram. She started slipping off her coat, but Daddy grabbed it before it left her shoulders.

"Put your coat back on, Ma, and stop this." He said

it through teeth that met together so tightly it couldn't have been his natural bite. "I've had a long day, I need my dinner, and we're all going out for a good time."

I was impressed by how Daddy had summarized everything like that. We were learning to summarize in school, and I wasn't very good at it yet. He was just a whiz.

Everyone else seemed impressed, too, because they all started to file out the door as quietly as could be. No one even noticed that I'd put a heavy sweater on Leland and one of the woolen hats Daddy and I had bought three for a dollar. Mama acted as if it were the most natural thing in the world for Leland to show up in the back seat of the car all dressed for snow.

Everybody was real polite in the restaurant. Gram said how light the biscuits were and Mama said how they were almost as light as Gram's; Daddy let Leland drizzle as much honey onto his biscuits as he wanted. There were little pots of fake holly on each table and colored lights in the windows. There was a big picture of Santa Claus in his sleigh over the door inside.

"How many more days?" asked Leland when we drove home past the tree on the green.

"Well, let me see . . ." said Mama.

"Ten," I answered. It was three more days until Christmas vacation and another week after that till Christmas.

"That's a long time," said Leland.

"Not so long," I told him. "Mama and Gram are gonna take you to the talent show the day after tomorrow. Wouldn't you like to see it?"

"I guess so."

"Martin Blumberger is gonna bring his dog that does tricks."

"I'd like to see that."

"What do they call her?" asked Gram. "The dog?"

"Trixie."

"Doesn't take much imagination to come up with a name like Trixie for a dog that does tricks. I hope his act has more going for it than that."

"I'll bet he's real good," said Mama. I appreciated her saying that. "And I'll bet you'll be real good, too, honey." She gave my hand a squeeze.

"Good at what?" asked Gram. "What's Mary Francis so good at? What's she doing in a talent show?"

"She's playing her accordion," Mama said real slowly like she was making an announcement.

"You're not!" said Gram. I think she was truly surprised.

"I'm a lot better than I used to be, Gram. You never really listen when I practice. I've improved a whole lot."

"I surely hope so."

"Now what kind of encouragement is that, Ma?" said Daddy. "Mary Francis is very brave to volunteer to play in front of a whole auditorium full of people in a brand new school."

I'd never thought about it that way. I wondered if it had been a big mistake to sign up.

"And you'll do just swell, honey," said Mama. "Won't she do just swell, Leland?"

"Sure you will, Mary Francis."

"Why, we came all this way just to see for ourselves, didn't we Leland?"

"I guess so, Mama."

Why was she saying a thing like that? Was it for Gram's benefit? Had she forgotten our telephone conversation? Was I supposed to play along?

When we came alongside the river, you could hear it roar even through the closed car windows.

"I have a bad feeling about that river," said Mama out of the blue.

"You said it was beautiful."

"And it is. It just takes my breath away. But it's dangerous, too. My sixth sense tells me that."

"What sixth sense?" Gram asked. It was pitch black in the car, but I just knew she was sneering.

"You know all about my sixth sense, Ma. I'm not going to discuss it."

"Mama's clairvoyant," I said.

"Of course she is," said Daddy. He put his arm around her and she scooted close to him.

"I'll give you clairvoyant," said Gram. She gazed into the dark. "I've got this strong feeling that we're going to have a crash-up if Forest doesn't take a look at the road and put his two hands back on the wheel. How's that for sixth sense!"

"I'm in complete control, Ma," said Daddy, but Mama slipped from under his arm and moved away.

"She's probably right, sweetheart." She giggled. "This is no time to be pitchin' woo. We're not sixteen anymore."

"There's been a whole lot of water under the bridge since either one of you was sixteen. Your own child will be old as that in a few years."

Most of the time I didn't feel like I was close to that old or like I was a child either. I hadn't felt like a child since Leland was born. He became the child as soon as they brought him home from the hospital. And Mama. Mama was a child sometimes. I was just who I was from one day to the next. If I had to put words to it, I'd say I was always in the process of becoming something or someone . . . too old for some things and too young for others. I just was.

CHAPTER TEN

THE WRANGLING DIDN'T START UP AGAIN UNTIL Leland's bedtime. I was supposed to be doing my homework, but everybody seemed to assume that I'd put him to bed like I used to. He never owned a pair of real pajamas in California, so I couldn't believe it when I found some brand-new Doctor Dentons with feet in his little suitcase. When he put them on, he looked just like some kid on the cover of *The Saturday Evening Post*.

Daddy had agreed he could sleep in the top bunk, if the railing was up. Once Leland climbed the ladder and squirmed under the covers, he was out like a light.

As I started back down the hall to the kitchen table where I'd left my books, they were at it again. So I turned around, dressed for bed in the dark, and sat in the stiff chair by the window. The mill was quieter and darker than usual. The stars were like bright pebbles you could pick out of the sky.

Gram was yelling now, really yelling. And Mama was crying. I could hear Daddy stomp over to the radio and turn it on too loud so it would cover everything up.

Somebody upstairs was pounding on the floor, and Mrs. Feingold had begun rapping on the water pipe. But turning up the volume like that was what Daddy always did just before Mama or Gram began to say things that could really hurt. I didn't want to hear even the bits and pieces of it. I put my fingers in my ears and looked at the stars again. They were always in the same place. You could depend on the stars.

I wondered what it would be like to be outside all the time like that, to be so brilliant everyone was bound to notice, to be immovable, to be cushioned by nothing but dark sky. Could my spirit move from a small room like this one out into all that space? It had been really hard to come back last time. Would that happen again?

When Mama started down the hall sobbing, I just had to get away from it. It was more than I could bear.

This time it was swifter than any other, and there was no sensation of moving through walls or the window screen or anything. All at once the spirit part of me was existing in some enormously restful place. It wasn't a cold place. It wasn't even especially dark. The amazing thing was that I hadn't really left Leland behind. From wherever I was, I could hear every little squirrel breath he took in his sleep. And I hoped that if he called out, I'd be able to just uncurl from the chair by the window as though I'd been sitting there all along.

When he didn't call, I began to be aware of how

comfortable it might be to just lose myself out here. At the same time I realized little by little that I had no way of telling where my spirit began or ended. Just as before, there were no boundaries or ways to define the space it filled, a space so undemanding and rootless it seemed to be the one perfect place where I belonged.

Yet, after a while, like the wings of some trapped moth, there came this faint stirring of my old unsettled feelings, then a growing urgency and need to get back to something solid, to things and people that I knew and loved. When it seemed that everyone must be in bed, I willed myself back into the chair, concentrating as hard as I could on a speedy trip. All I could manage, however, was to drift back very slowly and fitfully. It was such a rough and bumpy ride that at one point I started wondering if I'd ever break away from whatever was holding me. Though the leaving was getting easier every time, it was getting harder and harder to return.

"You went to bed awful early," said Mama in the morning. Her eyes were puffy and red and she was still in her bathrobe. Daddy had already left.

"I was tired, Mama."

"You know, it wouldn't have hurt you to stay around and stick up for me." She poured milk into her coffee, which looked cool already. There wasn't any steam. "I count on you to do that, Mary Francis."

"I was putting Leland to bed."

"I know that, honey. But then you never came back. You just disappeared."

"I told you, Mama. I was really tired."

"Don't pretend you didn't hear anything." She gave this kind of tragic laugh and shook her head. "You'd have to be deaf not to have heard anything."

I poured corn flakes and canned grapefruit juice and sat down across from her. I could feel her eyes on me while I ate. When I looked up, she looked away.

"I don't want to take sides, Mama," I said. "I don't even know which side to be on anymore."

Mama looked as if she was going to start crying again.

"I can't believe this, Mary Francis. I thought surely you'd see my way of thinking. I thought you loved Leland."

"Of course I love Leland, Mama. But that doesn't mean I think it's such a good idea for you to make him into a movie star."

"I get it. It's some brother-sister rivalry," said Mama. "I hadn't expected it, but here it is, clear as day. That's it, of course. That's why you're not on my side."

She was wrong. I wasn't feeling anything like rivalry.

"I just miss you, Mama. I miss Leland, too. It's no good having you three thousand miles away. I don't like us all being so far apart."

"Is that how far it is? Well, my goodness. I hadn't figured it out exactly."

But I don't like the fights either, I thought. Having us all in one place wasn't working out so well.

I changed the subject.

"Tomorrow's the talent show."

"So soon? Have you practiced? Are you sure you know your music?"

I hadn't been able to practice since she'd arrived. And I'd never be able to get to Rollo's Roller Rink without her noticing. I'd just have to hope I'd worked hard enough before and that it would all come together somehow.

She turned happy, like she'd flicked some switch from black to white.

"Do you have something fancy to wear?"

I hadn't even thought about that, about what I'd wear.

She grabbed my hand and pulled me up out of my chair.

"Let's look in your closet."

Leland was still asleep, but he didn't even stir.

There were three dresses that fit me in my closet, the two that Gram had made me for school and the deep blue velvet dress Mama had splurged on last Christmas so we could have our pictures taken for a family Christmas card. She'd bought Leland a velvet suit, too. That was when we were sure we were rich and we didn't have a thought in the world about moving out of Beverly Hills, let alone of doing it piecemeal like this.

"Try it on, sweetheart, so Gram can adjust it if need be."

Gram wasn't going to want to adjust it. She hated the dress. She'd said how it was a disgrace to spend so much on something to wear when there were people out there living from hand to mouth. But I didn't want Mama mad at me again, so I slipped it on over my nightgown.

"Perfect," she said. "It fits just perfect."

To me it seemed tight across the chest and under the arms, and it was a little too short. But there wasn't anything else I could wear, so I didn't mention it. From a distance, from out in the audience, maybe it would look like it fit.

Mama seemed to have stopped worrying about whose side I was supposed to be on. As soon as Leland started rubbing his eyes and yawning, she told me to go fix his breakfast while she did her hair.

When I left for school, Gram's door was still closed.

On the way home, I stopped at Rollo's Roller Rink to see if I could rent shoe-boot skates overnight. The man at the desk—Rollo, I think—knew me by now and said it wouldn't be a problem, if I could get them back by the next afternoon.

"Don't go using them on any city streets. Those are indoor skates," he said. As I started out the door he called, "Hey, kid. Where do you plan to use those skates?"

"At school," I said.

"School, huh? Where in school?"

"The auditorium," I said. "The stage."

He'd never understand if I tried to explain the rest of it.

I wasn't very hungry at dinner. We had the meat loaf meant for the night before and canned peas and big baked potatoes with butter — all things that I liked. But butterflies started up in my stomach whenever I thought about my performance. I hadn't even run through it once from start to finish. What I really needed was to practice on the stage before school. To do that, I'd have to get there extra early, after the school had been unlocked, but before anyone else was inside. If I got a ride from Daddy, it would be early enough, and I could make him think it was so I wouldn't have to carry my accordion all that way.

"But won't you be waiting around an awful long time, Mary Francis? Will any of the teachers be there?"

I hadn't any idea.

"Oh, sure," I said.

At 7:30 in the morning, I lifted my accordion from the back seat along with the paper bag with the skates in it and plunked them onto the sidewalk. I shut the car door and called "Bye" like I was on my way to join a crowd. Then I picked everything up again, chugged up the front stairs, and waved at the top. Daddy waved back and took off. I tried the front door even though I knew it would still be locked. It was a little easier going down the stairs with my heavy load and around the building to the playground.

The benches were cold as ice, so I put all my things on one but I sat on a canvas swing and turned and turned to keep warm. When I leaned way back, I could see that the sky was gray as slate. A fuzzy sun was almost lost in the clouds. A flock of black crows flew in ragged lines just above me. There was loud cawing coming from a crow roost in a tree across the street and a raspy sound from the swing's chain. Everything else seemed so quiet, like a big field of silence that needed to be filled with sounds. It would be. And then it would become a different place. It was a puzzle how things changed around you even if you stayed in the exact same spot. I was thinking how nice it would be to keep this place just the way it was, how all the kids could go around speaking in whispers, when the janitor came from the other side of the building jangling a ring of keys the size of a small dog collar. He tried a few in the basement door below the auditorium before pushing it open with two hands and disappearing inside.

I wasn't quick to follow. I wondered if I'd be able to find my way to the stage from the basement. I wondered if the janitor would throw me outside when he saw me. But I had to get in somehow.

When I tried the same door he'd used, it seemed

locked as tight as the front one. But then I remembered how he had pushed on it. I put my accordion down and pressed with all my might and it flew open.

Inside was a narrow passageway with one yellow bulb just bright enough so I could make out a few stairs at the end. On my way to them, I kept bumping back and forth from one wall to the other with the weight of my accordion. And holding the skates on top with my chin made my neck hurt. When I came to the stairs, I could see that there was a whole set of them heading straight up. Another door was at the top and it was closed.

I put my load on the floor, ran up the stairs, and turned the knob. What perfect luck! On the other side was the backstage area, speckled with light from high windows. It was almost too easy. It was anything but easy getting my accordion and skates up the stairs with no railing, though. When I'd finally made it, I collapsed on the dusty floor to catch my breath. Where had the janitor gone? There was no one here. I had the place to myself.

I sat on a pile of what looked like scenery to lace up the skates, strapped my accordion over my arms, and began to glide. The heavy dark curtains were closed, so I skated in the space behind them. Under my feet was a big smooth wooden rectangle of stage. It would be a snap.

Although, with the drapery shut, the space was cramped, I got the hang of it right away. As one foot kept rolling, the other one would rest, and I could play an entire phrase on the keyboard with one hand while pushing the air in and out with the other. That's the way it went from one side of the stage to the other — glide, play and push, glide. Back and forth, back and forth, just like the swan in the piece I'd chosen as my first number. Of course, I couldn't see myself, but I felt really graceful, and it had to be pretty interesting, especially when I was gliding with my leg out and the audience was looking up at me. The dress was a little tight, but I'd expected that. I was sure that people around here had never seen a dress made of velvet like this one.

When I started to play the Tarantella, I couldn't pull things together at first. The music had a fast, dancing rhythm, so I had to speed everything up. For this piece, I saved the part where I stick my leg out until the very end, when I play a couple of final chords. It seemed to work. I didn't fall over or anything. It was going to be great.

By the time I'd run through both selections twice and tried skating backwards in places, I could hear the other kids starting to arrive on the playground. I left my accordion and skates backstage, out of sight. Mama was going to love it. She was going to be amazed.

CHAPTER ELEVEN

AFTER THE ACTUAL PERFORMANCE WAS ALL OVER, I kept running it over and over in my mind. It had started out just the way I'd expected. The student body president, Harry Oglesby, introduced me right after Miriam and Her Talking Bird and before the Monroe School Bell Ringers under the direction of Harry Oglesby's mother.

Harry had just announced Mary Francis and Her Skating Accordion when the curtains parted (Elsbeth had that job), and there I was. I stood still for a minute to give everybody the full effect. Mama, Leland, and Gram were in the front row, and I could see the impact on them right away. Mama was squinting at the skates like she must be seeing things. Leland had his wide-open smile. Gram gave this what-do-you-know! kind of look. The little bit of laughter coming from behind them sort of confused me, but I started right in.

Back and forth, back and forth. Everything was going just the way I'd planned. I glided off with my leg out. I glided back. I went backwards; I went forwards. I felt just like a swan. I remembered every note.

It happened before the Tarantella, just as I decided to make use of the full stage. With the curtains pulled back, it seemed that I should use all the room I could get. But as I threw myself into the music and motion, instead of gliding straight out, I suddenly hit a surprise bump in what had looked like an entirely smooth place, and I went straight up. I came down in the exact same spot, hurting from the fall and flattened by the weight of my accordion and my sudden shame. Worst of all, there was a loud rip as I slowly rose to my feet and tried to continue. I began to feel a cold draft all along my back, but I skated on. Waves of laughter drifted up at me like a background chorus for the notes I was still trying to play.

I knew I shouldn't give up, but if I'd ever wanted to leave a terrible situation, this was the time. I suddenly remembered how a little spiritual trip had been part of my original plan when Gram had suggested the accordion and roller skates combo back in California, and before I could even decide whether the trip was still a good idea, I was out of there. At least my spirit was out of the performance itself, though I kept watching every move from someplace where I had a very good view. And strangely, as soon as I left, everything seemed to come together. I could hear all of it or nothing, just as I chose. The music began to make sense, the skating got more interesting and intricate, the laughing all but stopped, but I was terrified that I wouldn't be able to get back in time.

When the skating and playing Mary Francis finished, there was loud applause and she was bowing all over the place. My spirit, however, was tugging for dear life against the mysterious something trying to hold it back. It was wrenching itself away with every bit of strength that it possessed, finally inching back into my body as sluggishly as thick molasses poured onto a spoon.

"You were just wonderful," said Mama as she gave me a great big hug afterwards. "It was a little bumpy at first, but when you got over the jitters, you were an astonishing spectacle up there. Just astonishing."

"How'd you learn to do that, Mary Francis?" asked Leland.

"It was my idea," said Gram. "I knew you could do it. I just didn't expect as how you'd be that good. I never would have dreamed!"

"Too bad about the dress," said Mama. "It isn't as though you just ripped a seam or anything. You tore this great big hole right down the middle."

"Thank the good Lord you had on clean underwear," Gram added. "It's a good lesson to us all."

I didn't understand about the lesson, but I did know one thing: they were all proud of me.

"Too bad your Daddy couldn't get away to see you," said Mama.

I was wishing he had been there, too, but it didn't matter so much. He appreciated me no matter what I did.

And I was also wishing I'd been just a little clairvoyant myself, that I'd had some forewarning of how what I'd done that afternoon was going to complicate matters. The first thing out of Gram's mouth when we got home set the stage for a whole new series of upsets.

"Now that it's clear as day you've got two talented children, Loreen, are you going to continue to concentrate on one and not the other?"

Mama became flustered.

"Well, proud as I am of Mary Francis's achievement, Ma, I don't believe that what she does, that her accordion routine, could put her in the movies."

"And I'd say you're playing favorites."

"That's not it at all!" She tossed her dark hair and put a finger on her smooth cheek with one thumb under her chin as if she was thinking. "Do give me credit for knowing a thing or two about the industry by now. We've been knocking on enough locked doors."

"Locked doors?" I asked.

"Just an expression, sweetheart. I mean, I know how hard it can be. And Mary Francis is at that awkward age—not a child and surely not a woman. If I can't sell a darling little-boy dancer, what chance do I have with an in-betweener musician type?"

What a horrible description of me, of my talent. I knew she wasn't trying to be mean. She just couldn't think of any other way to describe it.

"Don't you worry, Mary Francis," Gram said to me. "The day that vaudeville comes back, you'll be right in your element. Your mama will be sorry she didn't see the possibilities in you."

When Daddy got home and they told him about my performance, Gram started in again. This time he retreated behind his newspaper and refused to join in. As I went to kiss him goodnight he said, "To work up a routine like that all by yourself, why, that takes talent, Mary Francis. And to keep going after a fall like the one you took, it takes a real trooper. Yes, a real trooper."

"And, Mary Francis," he called after me when I'd turned away, "you don't need the movies to make your mark."

I was glad he'd said all of it, but especially the last part because I knew Mama wasn't going to change her mind and because he was right.

What none of them knew was how my gift from Nora had been changing into something that pulled me away with increasing ease, how it had become this instant problem-solver, this refuge from everything I didn't like about myself or my life. But it had seemed to be much more than that for Nora. She'd planned her whole existence around it. I wanted it to be something more for me, too. And I wanted it to hold some answers to this separation that Mama wasn't about to bring to an end anytime soon.

If only I could ask Nora. If only I could be in touch. There was so much I needed to know, like how did she learn to go from one body to another? How did she choose the person for such an important switch? There wasn't anybody I could think of right offhand who I'd want to inhabit. Unless of course it was Mrs. Moran on our party line in Beverly Hills. When Mama and Leland went back there, I could visit in the wink of an eye if it was Mrs. Moran.

You might call it coincidence or sheer luck, but at the time I was sure that Nora had read my mind from wherever she was and put an answer in my path. Just days later, right before Christmas like it was a present or something, there was an unusual message on the little bulletin board at LeGrande's. I'd taken to reading the ads and things up there just for fun, but this particular message stuck out from all the others because of the stars and moons drawn all around the edge. I remember thinking how even Leland could have drawn better stars and moons, how he would have thrown in a few constellations. When I looked closely, it was the words that hit me, especially the first one—*spiritualist*. That was what Nora had called her religion, her church, and herself. I had thought she'd made it up. In scratchy block letters, the ad read:

SPIRITUALIST IDA MAE HANSON
INVITES ONE AND ALL TO HER
ANNUAL HOLIDAY SÉANCE AND CELEBRATION,
DEC. 27 AT 7:00 P.M.
GET IN TOUCH WITH DEAR DEPARTED LOVED ONES
AT THIS SPECIAL TIME OF YEAR. SING-ALONG AND
LIGHT REFRESHMENTS. CHILDREN MUST BE
ACCOMPANIED BY AN ADULT.

"What's a séance?" I asked Mr. LeGrande.

"Some mumbo jumbo where everybody sits around and talks to dead people. Nothing to interest a little girl."

At the bottom of the ad was a telephone number and address.

Could Nora be considered a loved one when I hadn't exactly loved her? I had liked her well enough. Yet I wondered if I might be excluded from the séance for lack of real emotion. Still how were they, how was Mrs. Hanson, going to measure a thing like that? I was pretty sure I could convince her of my attachment to my dear departed. I wouldn't have to fake it. I really needed Nora's help.

"Where's School Street, Mr. LeGrande?"

"Right there on the side of your own school. If it was a dog, it woulda bit you."

It would be easy to find the place — this was getting better and better. Of course, it was school vacation now, but I could think of some excuse to walk that way during the day. The problem was finding a good excuse for taking off at night and getting an adult to go with me. As it stood now, Mama and Leland were leaving on the day after New Year's. It didn't look like she was going to change her mind about that, so maybe I could get Mama to come with me to the séance.

CHAPTER TWELVE

THE NEXT TIME THAT MAMA AND GRAM WERE DEEP into one of their insult wars, I bundled Leland up and we went for a long walk. He didn't have galoshes like I did, he only had his school shoes, but there was just a dusting of snow on the sidewalks and the air was so cold and dry that the drifts lifted like smoke as we walked. Leland and I had been hoping for a whole lot more snow, but Daddy said there'd be more than enough before too long and we'd be plenty sick of it before winter was all over.

Leland was tired and cold by the time we reached LeGrande's, so we stopped for penny candy and took off our mittens to warm our hands by the wood stove. Mrs. LeGrande seemed real chatty all of a sudden. She wanted to know if I'd like to hear the story of her life. Mr. LeGrande said, "Not again, Elise," but she didn't listen to him.

"I was born and raised in Quebec City. You got that so far?"

"Yes," I said. What was there to get?

"I got married. You with me?"

I nodded.

"My husband, he move me to this godforsaken town where we got no friend, no family, nobody to speak French."

"And then what happened?" I asked, trying to sound interested.

"Nothing happen," she said in a sad and angry voice. "Oh, yes. I work and work and work."

"You don't want to forget that," said Mr. LeGrande. He lit his pipe and went out onto the steps

"Is that a good story or what?" asked Mrs. LeGrande. She pounded the counter with her fist.

I didn't answer her. Leland looked frightened. He tugged on my coat.

"We have to go now," I said.

"Sure," she said. "Run along."

She gave us each some horehound drops, turned her back, and started rearranging things on the shelves.

"She's homesick," said Mr. LeGrande as we passed him just outside the door.

"I'm sorry."

"She'll get over it. After Christmas. She'll be fine after Christmas."

I wondered if it was a place she was missing so much or the people in it. I knew I'd felt a lot worse when Mama had been so far away. I'd missed our back yard and the orange trees and the hot, dry summer days. With Mama and Leland here, I still missed those things, but I didn't feel sick. I knew that kind of sickness. I knew what it felt like. But I hadn't known that grownups felt it, too.

After we'd left LeGrande's, Leland picked up speed a little bit, but it was slow going with a six-year-old who had to look at every twig and gum wrapper on the way.

School Street was on the far side of the school, and the street dead-ended at Mill Street, the one at the front of the school. That was the street we lived on and the one we'd walked along to get here. There was only one direction we could choose, and the number I was looking for was nine, right in the middle of a long block. If I'd ever been by here before, I would have noticed the house for sure—the bright blue shutters, the little plaster elves all over the front yard. There were six or seven colorful birdhouses either on poles or hanging from leafless trees. And there were Christmas lights around the inside of the front window, turned on even in the middle of the afternoon, and heavy silver tinsel along the eaves. A garden gate in front was unlocked and swinging in and out on its hinges. The creaking in the quiet afternoon gave me goose bumps, but Leland put his feet on the bottom board and took a ride.

"That's not your gate, Leland. You can't go swinging on other people's gates."

He jumped right off the way I knew he would. I didn't like making him stop, especially when he didn't put up a fuss the way any other kid would. It was good

I'd said something, though, because there was a curtain pulled back and a face at the window for just an instant. We walked on before that person had time to get to the door, and we didn't look back. The face had been blurry, but the eyes had pierced like arrows.

Going home, we crossed over to the river side and were walking against the flow of the rapids. The air was actually still and light, everything that the water churning below and beside us was not. Leland threw sticks into the foam, and they were sucked away in a flash of white.

"Let's get closer," he kept saying, "down on the rocks."

Mama had said to be sure not to go to the river alone. Well, I wasn't alone. And we'd be careful. I wouldn't let him get too close.

The rocks had patches of wet snow and they were slippery in places. If I'd known it before we jumped down, I probably would have gone straight home. Leland's shoes weren't meant for climbing, and my galoshes had slick rubber soles.

"This is far enough," I said when we were still pretty near the road.

"Feel the spray, Mary Francis. I'll bet if we got just a little closer, we could really feel it." Leland scooted down on his bottom and leaned out.

I tried it, too. I loved the spray against my face, the way it made my hair curl up.

He dropped one mitten and it got caught on a scraggly bush growing right out of a lower outcropping of rock.

"Don't you move!" I shouted as he started to lunge for it. "Stay right where you are."

I scraped along on the seat of my pants, lowering myself from one rock to the next until I thought I was close enough to reach out and pull the mitten free. I held on to another branch with one hand and stretched out my other arm.

"It's too far out," called Leland. "You can't reach it from there."

I bent a second branch that looked dry enough to snap, but it was green in the middle. I twisted it, bent it again, tore at it for so long that it finally ripped free. Then I worked on the end to make a kind of hook and I leaned out again.

It seemed perfectly safe. I had a secure foothold and had anchored myself by clutching a tough little bush. I remember wondering how anything could grow like that right out of a rock crevice, how it could get enough nourishment with no soil. I was thinking how it depended on no one, how it must somehow manufacture all its own strength, when I realized that I'd begun to lose my grip. I was slipping. I was falling headfirst into the rapids.

I remember water shooting up my nose and the shock of the searing cold, and I remember surfacing farther downstream with one big *thud* as my side hit the rocky ledge. I grabbed wildly at a shriveled tree branch and held on with both hands. Leland's faint cries were coming from far behind me. I was facing away and couldn't possibly turn to see him.

"Hold on, Mary Francis!" I thought he called. There were tears and panic in his voice. "I'll go—" and I couldn't hear the rest.

Where would he go? Did he even know where he was exactly? Could he run on the snowy sidewalks?

With no flat place to pull up to and the water pressing me into hard rock, I continued to hold on. I had never felt cold like this. It was as if an icy spike had been driven right through the top of my head and clear down to my toes. But even as I was falling it had been obvious to me that there was a way to get away from this, to separate myself and rise above this disaster. I knew it would even be easy. The last time had taken just a need or a wish.

Yet somehow it seemed very, very important that I not do it this time. I knew that I should be entirely present in this crisis, that I must continue to experience the raw pain and fear of it so that I wouldn't distance myself from Leland. He was bound to return, with or without help. He needed to know that I—all of me—was all right and right here. There wouldn't be time for my spirit to come back as slowly as it had before. I didn't know if I'd even have the spiritual energy. I wouldn't want Leland to think even for a minute that I wasn't truly present. It would scare him half to death. Maybe I had fooled people who'd watched me from the distance of an audience, but I wouldn't be able to fool Leland.

Also, there was the awful thought that maybe this time my body would let go and be carried downstream and I'd never be able to catch up to it. In the past my body had performed more reliably when I'd released it, but I couldn't be absolutely certain it would do that this time.

I don't know how I had the physical strength to hold on for what seemed like forever, like hours instead of minutes. The thunderous noise of the water in my ears was all I was conscious of at times, the noise and this terrible effort against the pull of the current. The water wanted me to fail. The cold wanted me to sink right into it, to love it with all my might, to give in.

At some point I noticed that it was starting to get dark. A soft bronze film was settling over everything, and I wondered if anybody would be able to find me here in the dark. I wondered if Leland would recognize the spot where we'd decided to climb down, if he could point it out to someone else. What if Leland was lost now and wandering around? Would Mama know where to look for either of us? Had she begun to worry?

When I saw small circles of light moving over the rocks and the water's edge, I thought I might be dreaming or seeing things. The circles hopped about with the pace of someone walking very carefully but very fast. I heard a voice like a whining wind — no words, just a thin stream of sound that cut through the roar. I tried to call out but knew I couldn't make myself heard. My arms were aching and my hands were losing strength. My grip was slipping very, very slowly. The dark was closing in. I couldn't see more than a few feet in front of me.

Then I heard a word. One word: *There!* I was sure I'd heard it. And then a sentence. A whole, entire sentence. *She's down there!*

How was I able to hear Leland's small voice over all of this? How had he managed to come back and find me? In minutes I felt Mr. LeGrande's large hands under my arms. He was lifting me up, then prying my hands from the tree branch as quietly and surely as if he were a piece of machinery maneuvering a log. When he set me down on my feet, I couldn't stand up. There was no feeling in my legs at all. I felt like a solid block of ice. But he seemed to understand this and wrapped me in a rough blanket and carried me back up over the slick rocks, back to the road and to Leland, who was crying in big terrified gulps.

I couldn't speak yet. I wanted to tell him that he had done exactly the right thing, that getting Mr. LeGrande was the smartest thing he could have done. But every time I opened my mouth, my teeth chattered so much I couldn't say a word.

The LeGrandes closed the store and put me in front of the wood stove. Mrs. LeGrande took off my wet clothes, rubbed me down with dry towels, and wrapped me in a soft, dry blanket. Mr. LeGrande called Mama, who sounded hysterical over the phone even from where I sat huddled in a chair. He had to keep reassuring her that Leland and I were just fine.

"There's nothing to worry about, Madame," he kept saying. "I promise it."

As the blood started coming back into my feet and hands, I was in so much pain that I rocked back and forth and moaned even louder than Mama had when her hands were so cold. How long had I been in that water? I was still unable to ask.

"In the river much longer, young girl, and you would not be here to tell about it for sure," said Mr. LeGrande. He looked down at Leland. "You one fine hero, little fella, and some fast runner!" He turned back to me. "Your little brother run so fast, you maybe in that water ten, fifteen minutes tops."

Had it really been such a close call? Had it been as short a time as he said?

"I ran as fast as I could, Mary Francis. I knew we needed someone stronger than Mama to help us."

"Your mama is coming," said Mrs. LeGrande. "The visiting mama."

I thought that I could probably talk all right now, if I wanted to, but I didn't want to talk about that. When

I'd tried to explain it to kids at school, they either didn't understand or acted like I was making it up.

Leland and I were both drinking hot cocoa when Mama raced in the door in her high heels and thin coat. The expression on Mrs. LeGrande's face was disapproving and full of questions. Mama all but knocked the cup out of my hand while pushing my wet hair from my face and making sure with frantic pats and kisses that I was all in one piece. She picked up Leland and crushed his cheek against hers. She stood over me like some fierce guard.

"What did I tell you about that river? Didn't I sense something terrible about that river right off the bat?"

"Yes, Mama."

"Don't say I didn't warn you, Mary Francis. Didn't I warn her Leland?"

"I don't know," said Leland.

"Well, it doesn't matter now. All that matters is that you're all right." She looked around frantically for one of the LeGrandes; they were at opposite sides of the store. "She is all right, isn't she?" she called.

"She's a lucky girl," said Mr. LeGrande. "She could have drowned or died from cold."

Mama's face was drained of all warm color. It was blue as ice.

"I had no idea. I mean, I never imagined it was such a close shave as all that. Why, Mr. LeGrande, you saved my baby's life."

"This little guy," he said, patting Leland's head. "He's the one. Fast on his feet, this one."

"A dancer," said Mama proudly. "A professional dancer."

"The movie star," mused Mrs. LeGrande. Now it seemed to be making sense to her. "The movie star and the visiting mama." She didn't seem impressed. Confused, Mama turned her attention to Leland.

"Why, you deserve a prize, honey! A little boy who saves his sister's life deserves a prize. Isn't that right, Mary Francis?"

Of course I thought she was right. There was no prize good enough for what Leland had done. He was my brother and I loved him more than anything in the world.

When Daddy drove over to pick us up after work, Leland was holding a sack full of licorice cigarettes, Tootsie Rolls, and button candy and four of the newest Krazy Kat comic books. But it wasn't enough. It wasn't nearly enough.

CHAPTER THIRTEEN

WHEN WE GOT HOME, EVERYONE FUSSED OVER BOTH OF us for a while. Mama kept telling Daddy how they'd almost lost me, how it had been Leland's quick thinking and fast feet that saved me.

"And Mr. LeGrande, too," Leland reminded her.

"Yes, darling, of course Mr. LeGrande, too. But you were the one who had to race for help. Who would have thought those fast little feet and all those dancing lessons would have you saving lives?"

"One life," said Gram. "Just a one-ditch fluke. You can't be trying to justify all those expensive lessons on the basis of a one-ditch life-saving fluke! I mean, he's probably just a natural-born fast runner, and he isn't going to make a career out of saving lives left and right now, is he?"

But after they'd gotten used to the idea of my still being alive, I started to get it for climbing down to the river in the first place and for taking Leland along.

"I would have expected you to have more sense than that, Mary Francis," said Daddy. "Your mama warned you, after all."

"She said not to go there all alone."

"She was trying to save my mitten," said Leland.

"Which didn't get down there all by itself," Daddy reminded us.

"There were two of us. I thought it was okay with the two of us."

"I think you know I didn't mean to take Leland when I told you not to go there by yourself," said Mama. She gave me another big squeeze. "But I just can't scold you when I think how close we were to losing you. It makes me realize how much you still need your mama. It makes me just sick that I can't stay around."

Did she mean it? Did she really want to stay? Maybe falling in the river and almost drowning had been a really good thing.

She was still smoothing my hair and clucking over me when the phone rang and Gram answered it.

After listening a few minutes, Gram said, "Nobody here by that name," and hung up. "Funny thing," she said as she put down the receiver. "It was the long-distance operator and she was looking for somebody else named Leland. You hardly ever hear that name."

Mama dropped her arms to her sides and stood up straight. "Leland what?"

"One of those French-Canadian names. La something."

When the phone rang again, Mama all but pushed Gram out of the way to get to it.

"Hello, hello," she said, "Yes. This is the right number. Sorry about that little misunderstanding." She waited. "Yes. You've reached Leland LeBec. This is his agent, Loreen Ferguson."

Her pencil flew across the telephone pad while she kept repeating, "Um-hmmm. Um-hmmm. Yes. Twin Oaks 3221. Yes. I've got that. Mr. Siegle. Extension 253."

She was quiet for a long time. Gram had been hanging on every word and looking at Mama as if she must be deep in the middle of losing her mind.

"Of course," she said at last, "I'll have to check this all out with my client and get back to you. Darling Leland is busy with the celebrations of the season, and it may take some time."

When she finally put down the phone, Gram jumped right in.

"Leland LeBec? Who in tarnation is Leland LeBec?"

"I knew you'd be upset, Ma, if I told you. I knew you wouldn't understand how you can't be a movie star with a name like Ferguson, at least not Leland Ferguson. The name's too long and not a bit catchy. Leland LeBec—that's catchy as can be."

"Did you know about this, Forest?"

Daddy put the open paper down across his knees and looked up.

"About what?"

"About the fact your wife has gone and renamed your only son."

"Not renamed, Ma," said Mama. "LeBec is his stage name. Everyone does it. That little Sheila Grossman you met once? Well, she's Sheila Divine now. Isn't that cute? And you don't really think that Dorothy Lamour was ever really La anything do you?"

"It's not his legal name?" asked Daddy.

"Of course not, sweetheart. It's just, you know, a selling point. Something to make him stand out from the rest."

"I don't like it one bit," said Gram. "It's like you don't think Ferguson is good enough anymore. When I married George Ferguson, I thought it was the most beautiful name in the world. I wrote it all across the wall above my bed."

"How sweet," said Mama. "Isn't that just about the sweetest thing you've ever heard?" She nudged Daddy, who nodded and picked up his paper.

Then she said, "It's a fine name, Ma. You notice I didn't change my own." She whipped a card out of her purse on the table. "See. Doesn't it look just swell on this card? 'Loreen Ferguson, Movie Agent.' Isn't it something?"

"Why, you're no such thing! You should have put 'Movie Mother' down. That's what you should have put."

"Sometimes I don't think you understand one blessed thing about this business, Ma. I've told you before how they hate movie mothers. I've told you how it's the agents they revere." She looked real smug. "Well, now they can just go ahead and revere the heck out of me."

"If that doesn't take the cake!"

"I'm telling you, Ma. It works. Look how nice they talk to you on the phone. How polite they are when they think you're no relation."

"Sounds like a pretty smart move," said Daddy. He patted her on the backside. "Sounds like you're turning into a pretty smart cookie."

Mama sort of shimmied.

"Thank you, sweetheart. I knew you'd understand once I explained. I didn't mean to spring it on you."

"As long as it's not his legal name," said Daddy.

I thought he was being too easy on her, that she should have asked our advice or left it up to a vote or something.

"Do you like it, Leland?" I asked.

"Not exactly."

"Well. What exactly would you like better?" asked Mama.

"It's okay. I like it okay."

"You'll see, honey. It's working already! That was a callback from that audition we had two days before we left. Aren't you excited? Isn't that grand?"

"When do you have to go back?" asked Daddy, as if

this question were more important than any name change. "Do you have to go back any earlier than we'd planned?"

"I don't know yet for sure. I have to call this number and make an appointment."

She winked at him. "I'll try to put it off till as far after New Year's as I can."

"You've got to put it off till after New Year's!" I shouted. "We haven't even had Christmas yet. You only just got here." *And I thought you wanted to stay around. That you knew how much I need you.*

"I'll do my best. I can't promise anything else. You can't postpone the big breaks. You just can't do that, Mary Francis."

The big breaks. She'd been talking about the big breaks all my life. What were they exactly and how did you know them when they showed up? Were there any of them out there for me? They apparently didn't have anything to do with playing an accordion on skates or being saved from the rapids of a frigid, whirling river. It was plain as day, really, that they had everything to do with the movies and that Mama was spending all her time setting them up for Leland. If I was going to have to start finding my own big breaks, I'd have to look for them in my own real life without any help from her. When I thought about it, it had always been this way. Mama was going to make certain that Leland was a big success; if I was going to succeed at anything, it would be completely up to me.

When Mama called the number she'd written down, some man gave Leland an appointment two days after New Year's. It meant they'd have to leave the day after Christmas if they were going to get there in time. Leland staged the closest thing to a tantrum I'd ever seen from him. He cried and begged a little, then he climbed into his bed and wouldn't come out.

We didn't put up our tree until Christmas Eve, after Leland had gone to sleep. It was a tiny replica of the big one that last year had touched the ceiling of the house in Beverly Hills. All our regular decorations were still in the closet of that house, so it was a completely shrunk-down celebration.

Leland had been worried that Santa Claus wouldn't be able to find us, and since there wasn't any chimney he insisted we keep the front door unlocked. Daddy had done the Santa Claus shopping because Mama said she hadn't had time what with all the traveling. He didn't buy very much and didn't even wrap any of it. Leland got what he asked for, though — a Flexible Flyer. I got a very nice bed doll, the kind that has a fancy hat and long skirt and decorates your pillow. I guess Daddy had finally noticed I hadn't played with real dolls for years. Gram gave me embroidered handkerchiefs. You can't have too many of those. Mama wrapped up a silver dollar in a little silver box for me. She said how it was from the great gold rush state of California and how she'd had to go to the bank special for it before she left. I'd made fringed dresser scarves for everyone but Leland. I bought him a giant popgun, and he gave me a brand-new package of jacks all wrapped in cellophane.

We went to the Lithuanian church on Christmas day because it was the closest one, so we couldn't understand a word of the sermon. But there were carols and a manger and we were all together. It was a good Christmas, and I wanted to stretch out the time that Mama and Leland were still here, but somewhere inside I was anticipating the second day after Christmas. I was waiting for Ida Mae Hanson's holiday séance. The sing-along and light refreshments might be nice, too, but they were just the icing on the cake. The séance was the cake, and I was hoping for a great big piece.

CHAPTER FOURTEEN

IT SNOWED CHRISTMAS NIGHT, SO DADDY HAD TO PUT chains on the car tires for the long ride to see Mama and Leland off at South Station in Boston. This time I went along. The chains made an awful racket, and we moved along so slowly and carefully I wanted to jump out and run alongside. "Precious cargo," Daddy said when even Mama asked him if he couldn't speed up a little. She smiled at that and didn't bring it up again.

I'd never been on a train, and here was Leland, only half my age, taking his second train ride across the country in two weeks. He wasn't excited or anything. He didn't want to leave.

Christmas night I'd packed his things into his suitcase, making sure he had everything. I stuck some comic books in the bottom and gave him a separate bag to carry with more comics and all his presents except the sled. I knew Mama would forget things.

And even though I tried not to, as I watched them board the train, Mama first with Leland tagging along behind and Daddy lifting him up the steps, I worried that Mama wouldn't take good care of him, that she'd forget to put him to bed or to make him dinner, things like that. She'd slipped back so quickly into expecting me or Gram to take charge, but we wouldn't be there. It was a powerless feeling. What I wanted was to grab him off those steps and run away as far and as fast as I could. But I just stood there and watched as Mama leaned over to give Daddy one last long kiss and then posed with a knee bent and hand raised like some movie star getting ready to wave good-bye.

"You'd better find your seats," Daddy said sensibly, and we tracked their progress window by window as they made their way down the aisles of two passenger cars. When they finally got to their places and Leland pressed his face against the glass, he looked fishy and strange, as if he'd changed some in the minutes it took to get there. Mama stood over him and blew kisses for all the time it took the train to chug along and round the bend out by the flashing light.

When they were completely out of sight, Daddy put a hand on my shoulder and said, "I just wish I could have afforded to rent them a sleeping compartment. A berth's not nearly as comfortable as a sleeping compartment."

"Mama said she didn't care one way or the other," I reminded him. She had sounded like a little girl when she'd talked about what fun it had been to have the porter make up the beds for the night and how she'd loved to sleep behind the curtains.

"She's just being a good sport." He chuckled. "She's always such a good sport."

Was he talking about Mama? *Our* Mama?

I wasn't worrying one bit about her. I was wondering if Leland would get to run around at all, if there'd be anyone for him to play with, if I'd packed enough things to keep him busy, if she'd remember to buy him snacks and regular meals, if he'd wake up and call out for me in the night.

When we got home, I couldn't face going back into the apartment with only Gram and Dad inside, so I made a snow fort with the Murphy twins. I was feeling just the way I did two years ago when our dog, Goldy, ran away and never came back. I cried and cried then, but it didn't do any good. There'd been this lump in my chest for such a long, long time and now it was back.

On some kind of impulse I shot a snowball super hard at the back of Ike's neck, and he got so red in the face I thought he was going to bust for sure. "No fair," he shouted, running into his house crying.

"You never play fair, Mary Francis Ferguson!" Mike echoed. When he grabbed their shovel away from me and followed his brother, it was already getting dark and I had to go on up anyway.

Mrs. Feingold was sweeping snow from the entry as I opened the storm door. She gave me this soft, sad look. "Bet you're going to miss that cute little fella." She sighed. "And your mama, too."

I couldn't answer her. She was being so kind, but I couldn't open my mouth to tell her so. At the top of the stairs I called down, "Thanks, Mrs. Feingold," but I think she was already back in her apartment and didn't hear. Mrs. Krakas leaned over the railing and looked. Looking was the most she ever did.

Inside, Gram's machine was whirring away. Her head was down and yards of material were passing under the needle like running water. Daddy was lying on the divan with his feet up and his hands behind his head. He'd taken the entire day off to see Mama and Leland to the train, and now he didn't seem to know what to do with himself. I could smell spare ribs boiling in the big iron pot on top of the stove. You could hardly hear *Portia Faces Life* in the background on the radio. Things were a lot like they'd been a few weeks ago. But there was an emptiness now that hadn't been so immense before Mama and Leland's visit. Their absence seemed to be, right this minute, growing and spreading through the rooms like bread dough rising out of control. Did Dad feel it? Did Gram? Why was everyone just letting this happen? When would it end?

It wasn't until I was lying awake in the top bunk again and watching the moon rise that I thought of Ida Mae Hanson and her holiday celebration. *Tomorrow night,* I thought with a start. I hadn't begun to figure out a way to get there yet. Daddy and Gram would never let me go out after dark. And then again, the notice had clearly stated that an adult must accompany any child. What was I going to do about that?

I noticed that the moon had a transparent pink center that made it look like two moons blended into each other in a very spooky way. I wondered if Nora could see that moon or another phase of it from where she was. I wondered if she knew what I was planning and if she was right now getting ready to receive the message I planned to send and to send me her answer. I couldn't let her down. I couldn't let myself down. I had to find a way to get to Ida Mae Hanson's séance.

When my opportunity appeared, it surprised me so I almost didn't take advantage of it. It was at breakfast and I was stirring my Wheaties and milk around and trying to think. Daddy had left for work already, and Gram had decided to sit down across from me for a second cup of coffee. She pulled her bathrobe together at the top with one hand, smothering the freckles on her chest she always tried to keep covered.

"Seems awful quiet around here," she said as she swirled sugar into her cup.

"Yeah."

"Like some big wind blew through and swooshed right out."

I nodded, surprised by her clear description of it.

"What you have planned?" she asked.

What did she mean?

"You've got at least four days of Christmas vacation left. What do you plan to do with yourself?"

"There's this party," I said before I could stop myself.

The tiny lines at the edges of Gram's eyes pinched together.

"Well, isn't that nice! A party. Who gives parties around here right after Christmas?"

"Ida Mae Hanson," I said.

"One of your school chums?"

"Not exactly." How was I going to explain?

"She's a lady who lives near here," I said.

"Some stranger? What lady goes around inviting little girls to parties? What made you think I'd let you go?"

"She invited you, too."

"Me? Why in the world would some strange lady invite me to a party?"

"It's for the whole neighborhood, I guess."

"Oh," she said. But I could tell she was still quizzical.

"And just where does this lady live?"

"Near my school," I said. "In a pretty house with blue shutters and birdhouses in the trees. Just the kind of place you like."

"I do like those nice little Capes. I can just picture us in one of those little Capes. Does it have a fence?"

"A white fence with a gate."

"I like fences with gates."

"So you want to go to the party?"

"Just to see some white fence with a gate? I don't know this lady. I've never met her friends."

This wasn't working out. How was I going to persuade her to come with me?

"Let me tell you about this party," I began. "Ever heard of a séance?" She got pop-eyed real fast.

"Of course I've heard of a séance. Don't tell me this so-called party is really one of those. It must be some kind of mortal sin to go to one of those."

"Even if you just watch?"

"Well, I don't really know about that. But what would make you want to go to one in the first place?"

"Nora." I said. It was the truth. It wasn't all of the truth, but it was a big chunk of it.

"Well, I never. I thought you'd forgotten all about Nora. Why in the world would you want to get in touch with Nora?"

Get in touch. That was exactly what I wanted to do. Get in touch with Nora, find out some of her secrets. Learn what I needed to know so I could travel to Beverly Hills in the wink of an eye and make certain that everything was all right.

"I'm just curious," I said. "And there's going to be a sing-along and light refreshments."

"Hmmm. Light refreshments. Sounds kind of homey."

"It does? I mean, it does."

"I always did wonder what people did at a séance. Like you, I've always been kind of curious."

"Then you'll go?"

"Well, I wouldn't want it to count up as a mortal sin for either one of us."

"The catechism says you have to know you're doing something really bad for it to be a mortal sin. A séance doesn't seem so bad."

"It says that, does it?"

"And wouldn't you like to find out what happened to Nora? I mean what really happened."

"She died," said Gram. "It really happened. She really died."

"I mean what happened after that."

"I don't believe anybody knows for certain what happens after that."

She was getting me mad, but I didn't let on. "Then we could just go for the fun of it."

"I suppose it might be fun. Lord knows, except for Mrs. Feingold and the girls at the bolt end store, there's little enough socializing goes on around here. When the man comes by selling scissors and such, I sometimes have him sharpen my shears or a knife just to pass the time of day."

"Mama might have a fit if we go," I said to get her on my side.

"She would, wouldn't she? Your daddy, too."

This was starting to feel like an adventure. Imagine, having an adventure with Gram! The thought had never crossed my mind.

"What time is the . . . party?" she asked.

"Seven P.M. Seven P.M on the dot."

I added that last part because I didn't want to be late. Gram always had a problem getting places on time — even church.

"What do you suppose people wear to a séance?"

Why were grown-up women — even Gram — so concerned with what they wore every place on earth? I didn't think it made a hill of beans' difference what we wore, but I said, "Probably a nice dress," just to make her feel better and because it was a party.

"Just imagine! The two of us going to a Christmas séance and all."

She was becoming giddy with anticipation. I hoped she wasn't going to be disappointed or scared away or anything. I hoped she wasn't going to get cold feet at the last minute.

"What do we tell your father?" she asked, looking more devilish than I thought was probably good for her. I didn't want to lie to Daddy. But I didn't want him to tell us we couldn't go, either.

"Maybe if we just say that it's a party," I said. "Maybe that's all we need to tell him."

"What if he wonders why we're both invited?"

"He doesn't think of things like that. He'll probably be glad he can listen to *Fred Allen* instead of *Fibber Magee*."

"Is it a long walk? I don't know if I can walk so far in this weather. Will I need my galoshes? What about streetlights?"

She went on and on like that all day, asking all kinds of questions and not waiting for the answers. You'd think she'd never been out of the house after dark before. By dinnertime, she seemed to have forgotten we were going to a séance and kept talking about the party so sincerely that it was no trouble at all to convince Daddy.

"Sure you don't want a ride there?" asked Daddy as we put on our coats. "It's turning cold. Might be twenty degrees by morning."

Gram gave me a panic-stricken look, but I quickly answered, "It's not far. And we've been inside all day."

"Suit yourself," said Daddy.

When we opened the door to the street and its biting cold blasts, I wondered if I'd made a mistake. But I couldn't let Gram see me wavering. I took in deep breaths of icy air as if it were a spring breeze.

"For heaven's sake, let's get started," she said at last, and we took off toward LeGrande's.

The packed snow was crunchy under our feet and squeaked if you hit it just right.

The dirty mounds at the side of the road were lit by

the moon and shone blue. Only a few cars passed, their chains clanging like dull bells. The wreaths on the doors and the lighted trees in some windows warmed up the outside and made it feel safe. Sometimes a radio program drifted into the dark where it didn't seem to belong. Our breath hung in front of us like tiny white clouds.

By the time we got to LeGrande's, Gram was desperate to go inside and warm up. I hoped she wasn't planning to get all chatty with Mrs. LeGrande and make us late. But Mr. LeGrande was the only one in the store. He said that if we wanted to warm up on the way back, we'd better get there before nine, when he was planning to close.

It was like prying a mussel away from a rock trying to get Gram from that stove once she'd landed beside it. I showed her the clock, how it was fifteen minutes to seven already. I started out the door myself. When she didn't follow, I went back and pulled her up from the chair with two hands, pulled her right through the door and out onto the steps.

"What kind of a way is that to treat your grandmother?" she asked indignantly. "What's that Mr. LeGrande going to think?"

"We've still got a ways to go yet, Gram. They might not let us in if we're late. What if they've started everything up and they don't want to be interrupted?"

"Well I never saw anybody so excited about something so peculiar. A party is one thing, but a séance?"

"I thought you wanted to go. You said you were as curious as I was."

"I don't know as how I'm curious enough to freeze off my behind. I'm not at all sure I'm curious enough for that."

"If we walk faster, we'll be there in no time. You'll see."

"No time, she says. It takes no time at all to turn to a statue in cold like this."

"Then walk, Gram. Just keep walking."

I prodded her along until she shook my hand off her arm and began to hustle under her own steam.

"I must have been crazy in the head to agree to this," she muttered every few feet.

But she was moving. We were on our way again.

CHAPTER FIFTEEN

GRAM GOT REAL SHY WHEN SHE SAW THE HOUSE WITH its bright lights and stream of people arriving at the blue front door. I was encouraged to find there'd be others besides us at the séance. Though I'd been sure such a thing would be a big hit in Beverly Hills, I had no idea if it would be a popular event in a small New England town.

Ida Mae Hanson answered my knock and seemed relieved when she saw Gram come up from behind me.

"Why, I believe you're the only child we have here this evening," she said. "I would have had to send you home if you hadn't brought your grandmother. The spirit world can be quite unsettling to youngsters, you understand."

I didn't understand, but I nodded and shook her hand while Gram told her what a nice little place she had and moved on into the tiny living room to peer at the other folks like some kind of spy. I myself was trying to get used to my first up-close impression of Ida Mae Hanson, who was as thin as Nora had been fat — bony thin with protruding cheek and neck bones that made her look like a chicken without its feathers. Her loose clothing hung around her short body like bed sheets that might slip off, and she glittered and clinked with all kinds of beads and chains and trinkets. Even her fiery red hair seemed to glitter, and her red-rimmed eyes flared with so much energy it made me tired.

After that long walk, Gram and I were both hoping she'd get right to the refreshments, but that didn't seem to be her plan. When all the folding chairs in the room were filled, she put a CLOSED sign in the lighted window and motioned for us all to be still.

"See? We might have been locked out," I whispered to Gram while conversations wound down.

Ida Mae Hanson cleared her throat. She turned in my direction and raised her hands as if to calm some sea.

"Those of you who have traveled with me before know a little of what to expect."

"She's a wonder," said the dumpy little woman on Gram's right who had been twisting her fingers and bouncing in her chair. "Calls a spirit down from the sky just like it was some trick bird out of a tree."

"For the newcomers," continued Ida Mae, "I always provide a short introduction before the actual sessions of discovery." Her voice was deep, too big for her body.

Traveled; sessions of discovery— this was going to be right up my alley!

"The spiritualist's art is something that has been with us since the beginning of time. However, there have always been those among us more attuned to the world of the spirit than others."

As she spoke, her words seemed blown through hollow tubes. They whistled on the ends. They flew off.

"I am one of those so attuned. It is my mission and my desire to help those less attuned."

She paused.

"Do not expect results on your very first visit here. Surprising things do happen, but we must go slowly. And we must all be willing to encourage the spirits related to others in the group to appear. These very spirits may have messages from our own dear ones who cannot, for one reason or another, make an appearance."

"We're going to *see* these spirits?" Gram blurted out.

Ida Mae seemed taken aback. "Well, no. Appearance in this case has more to do with a felt presence, a spoken message, which may in fact be transmitted across the great divide through the instrument of a living voice."

"You mean through one of us?" asked Gram.

Ida Mae Hanson was actually getting testy.

"No, Madame. More than likely it would be through me." She glared at Gram. "Usually it is the children whom we need to contain," she added through clenched teeth.

"Sorry, Reverend," said Gram. "I just don't want to

be caught off guard when one of us starts speaking in tongues."

"None of us will be speaking in tongues here. And I must remind you that I am not a reverend. You are confusing my services with those of someone from a religious denomination."

"Our spiritualist relation, Nora, called her place a church. She held church services."

"Madame," said Ida Mae Hanson, "I do not know this Nora person to whom you refer. There are as many kinds of spiritualists as there are birds of the air. I expect your Nora was in a class by herself."

When Gram tried to explain, Ida Mae held up her hand like a shield.

"We must nip these interruptions in the bud. I demand silence before we can begin. I will have it or we will adjourn."

"Don't get your dander up," Gram muttered, but she was blushing now and keeping her head low as if she were ashamed of her own outbursts. Ida Mae had put her in her place for a little while anyway. There was a buzz of annoyance.

"I wish to direct your attention to the fact that there are no tables here, no mirrors, no props of any kind. I do require that you hold the hand of the person on either side of you so there will be one unbroken chain of psychic energy. And I ask that you shut your eyes and listen only to the sound of my voice."

I could tell Gram was skeptical by the way she was looking up now from underneath her lowered lids.

"But first," Ida Mae said, just as we began to grope for other hands, "we will pass the plate for a freewill offering. Give whatever you can, whatever would make your loved one feel proud."

"I didn't bring my purse," complained Gram.

I didn't own a purse, but my silver dollar from Mama was tied into a handkerchief from Gram and making a little bump in my pocket. When the plate passed in front of us, I untied it and let it go. It was my best present. It was something Mama had gone to a lot of trouble to get just for me. And there it went, whisked away on a plate in seconds just so Nora would feel proud.

"Thank you, my friends, for your great generosity," Ida Mae said as the plate came into her hands. "Now." She sighed so loudly I thought that maybe she was taking off right then and there. "Would someone please turn down the lights? Would you all reach out for the hand of your neighbor?"

There were a couple of clicks before all the lights finally went out. It had been so bright, and now we seemed plunged into a black pit. But soon, because of the lights in the window, it became easy to make out where Ida Mae was amid the little bunches of people strung together like beads. She seemed to glow in the dark. It was restful, really. And holding Gram's hand felt okay, but it was really awful holding the hand of the sweaty little man next to me. Besides being hot and damp, his hand had such calluses that every time he made an involuntary twitch, it felt as though my fingers were being slashed. I hoped this hand holding would be over with soon. We'd been told to keep our eyes shut, but I thought I'd better watch closely the first time around, at least until we got the hang of it.

It was quiet for a long time. Someone's stomach rumbled, somebody burped, and someone else giggled. I wanted to, also, but I figured Ida Mae Hanson was upset enough at Gram.

Suddenly Ida Mae's hollow voice started in again.

"I'm seeing the name Joseph. Someone named Joseph is trying to get through to us. Is there someone here who needs to get in touch with Joseph?"

"How about Jesus and Mary?" Gram whispered to me, but Ida Mae heard her.

"Anyone who sees something amusing in all of this may leave. The spirits will not come to a place where they will be laughed at. There is not space in this room for anyone determined to make jokes."

I squeezed Gram's hand hard enough to make sure she got my message. If she spoiled this for me, I'd never forgive her.

After what seemed like forever, the man next to me spoke up.

"I . . . I . . . have something to say to . . . someone

named Joseph. Joseph Abermarle. Is that who you are?" he called. "Are you Joseph Abermarle?"

He stood up and let go of my hand, thank goodness. But then he sat down again and grabbed it back.

"Joseph," intoned Ida Mae. "Do you have something to say to this man?"

"I thought you'd be in hell for sure, Joseph," said the man in a very agitated way. "Is that where you are? Are you coming to us from hell?"

There was a low groan.

"And are you in torment, Joseph?"

The man got so fidgety, it felt as if his hand was cutting mine to ribbons.

Another groan.

"Good enough for you, Joseph," said the man. "Steal another man's wife, take away his business. What do you expect? If you're in hell, Joseph, now I can rejoice. I can rest easy at last."

The man put both fists to his eyes and began sobbing what I guessed were tears of joy.

"Oh dear!" said Ida Mae. "Joseph is leaving us. The vibrations are become fainter and fainter." She paused. "Oops! Joseph is no longer here."

She bent toward the group.

"You see, the spirits know when the atmosphere is unfriendly. They may stay away altogether if it is hostile. I suggest we strive for a more loving interchange this time. The little girl among us — do you wish to contact someone from the other side? Your mother, perhaps? A dead friend?"

"My mother is on her way back to Beverly Hills," I said. "But there is someone special I need to contact."

"A name. I need a name. A first name will do."

"Nora."

"Her? That Nora person related to your grandmother?" Ida Mae's voice had become shrill.

"That's the one."

"Well, I don't really know about her. I mean, it seems to me we might have . . . conflicts of interest."

"You mean, there might be some kind of competition going on?" asked Gram.

"Spiritualists do not compete, Madame. I merely meant that she and I might inhabit different . . . spheres, so to speak."

"It wouldn't hurt to give it a shot," said Gram. "I mean here you've got this little girl and her grandmother come all this way on this cold night."

"I fully appreciate your, er . . . sacrifice," she said. Then her voice thickened and her words speeded up. "But I'm not having any more truck with your smart lip." She cleared her throat again. "In other words, I'm not prepared to endure any more heckling if the results are not to your liking, silver dollar or no silver dollar."

She'd noticed!

"She'll be good," I promised.

"Then let's have quiet again. *Please!* Things are getting completely out of hand. How can I concentrate with these constant interruptions!"

It was so still after that I could hear my own stomach flopping around.

"Nora," said Ida Mae Hanson at last. Then she started chanting the name over and over again until I was afraid it would put me to sleep. When she stopped abruptly, there was a strange clatter and a loud pop. Someone gave a little scream.

"Nora," said Ida Mae again. "Are you here with us, Nora? If you are, give us a sign."

There was a slight tapping on the roof.

"Well, I'll be," said Gram. "That's a sign for sure. Nora's husband, Fred, was a roofer. Repair Your Roof Without a Ruckus — that was his motto."

"Silence!" said Ida Mae. Then, "I'm feeling pressure, immense pressure. A large spirit is entering this room. A very large spirit."

"That's her," yelled out Gram. "In life she was fatter than Aunt Jemima and Kate Smith put together!"

"One more outburst, Madame, and you will be extirpated."

Whatever that was, it sounded pretty horrible. I squeezed Gram's hand even harder this time and she slumped down into her seat.

"Have you something to say to Nora, little girl?"

"My name's Mary Francis."

"Mary Francis, have you some message for this poor, wandering spirit?"

"Ask her why she's poor and wandering," whispered Gram.

I gave her a quick kick.

"I have got a message," I said. "It's more like a question. I've got a question."

"Speak," said Ida Mae. "Nora is waiting to be in touch."

"First, it would help if all these people weren't here."

"Oh, for the love of Pete," said Ida Mae. "Where do you expect them to go? This is a séance, sweetie. There are always people at a séance."

"Okay," I said. But I wasn't too happy letting all these strangers in on my most private secrets. If only Nora and I had worked out some code like the one on the Orphan Annie ring with the special protecto feature. You could get it with ten Ovaltine labels, but Leland and I could never seem to drink all that Ovaltine.

"Hey, Nora," I said. "Hey, if you're around here now like we think, there's something I've just been dying to know. I mean, I want to know it without dying to find out." I was surprised at my own nervous laugh and hoped Ida Mae didn't think I was trying to make a joke.

A strange sound floated out of Ida Mae and quivered above me. It wasn't a *yes* or a *no* or any other ordinary word. It was a thrum. A nice kind of thrum that made it seem okay to go on.

"You left before I could ask this, but it's important that I find out. Actually I *need* to find out now. I get all that stuff about leaving the body, you see, but what I don't get, what isn't at all clear, is how to trade places with somebody else. I mean how did you get from your dining room into Lillian in San Francisco? How can I get from our apartment here in Hardenville into Mrs. Moran in Beverly Hills? Oh—and back, too. I'll need to come back." I didn't want to get stuck somewhere in between.

There was complete silence. No thrumming or roof tapping. Nothing at all.

"That's the most garbled message I ever heard," said Ida Mae. "I don't see how Nora or anyone else would ever be able to figure that out. Has anyone an inkling what this child is talking about?"

"Mary Francis Ferguson," I corrected her. "And Nora will know just what I mean," I said. "You've got to give her some time."

"We are prepared to wait five minutes for Nora's answer."

"Five minutes!"

"In the world of the spirit, time knows no bounds."

"Maybe time doesn't know any bounds," said Gram, "but I know Nora, and she doesn't take to being hurried."

What if Nora refused to leave in five minutes? What if she insisted on hanging around?

"How've you been, Nora?" I asked, trying to sound as casual, friendly, and welcoming as possible. "What's been going on up there or wherever?" Being family and everything, I had thought she might be a little more overjoyed to see us. A whoop and a holler might be a little too much to expect, but I was hoping for something more than this. I bet Gram was as disappointed as I was.

"No more chitchat, child," warned Ida Mae. "Just get the spirit's answer and move on."

The thrumming had encouraged me so. But nothing came on its heels. There were no interesting sounds now, just scuffling, coughs, and other restless noises. The man next to me let go of my hand again, and I cushioned it in my lap like a wounded puppy.

Suddenly there was a noise like wind in a chimney and loud scratching as if some cat had gone mad. Then there was a high, almost inaudible drone that was clearly not from a living person. It was so full of the very essence of all that I remembered of Nora that I felt feverish and reckless.

"Alas, Nora's spirit is leaving us," said Ida Mae. "It is rising higher and higher. It is struggling to be free of this room."

"Don't go yet!" I yelled, convinced now that she had been here and was slipping from my grasp. "Your five minutes isn't even up. And you haven't told me what I need to know! Nobody else can help me, Nora. You said I had the gift, remember? It's up to you to give me the missing pieces."

"She is lifting. She is on her way."

I jumped up, but Gram tried to pull me back down.

"Oops!" said Ida Mae. "She is gone."

"Wait!" I shouted up at the ceiling. "There's going to be a sing-along!" I remembered Gram telling me how Nora loved to sing "Washed in the Blood of the Lamb," but it was too late. Ida Mae Hanson was already snapping the lights back on and clapping her hands.

"Intermission," she announced. "Refreshments will now be served in the dining room."

"Not a minute too soon, if you ask me," said Gram.

But I wasn't hungry anymore. And I wasn't planning to stick around for the second half. As far as I was concerned, the evening had been a complete failure. Oh, Nora had come here from someplace just as I'd hoped. She had been here all right. But she had left without helping me one little bit.

CHAPTER SIXTEEN

I COULD CONVINCE GRAM TO LEAVE EARLY ONLY BY reminding her that LeGrande's would close at 9:00. I knew she couldn't imagine walking home without a stop by that stove. She wasn't as talkative on the way there as I'd expected. It wasn't until we were almost home that she said anything at all.

"To tell the truth, Mary Francis, it's not too clear even to me what you were going on about in there. Why in the world would you want to trade places with some old lady who wears two hearing aids and sleeps all afternoon?"

"It doesn't matter now anyway," I said. "I mean, if Nora couldn't or wouldn't tell me how to do it—"

Gram interrupted me. "I think it must have been Nora, though, don't you? The roof tapping was a dead giveaway."

"At first I thought it was just a big tree branch. There are lots of trees around that house."

"And the way Ida Mae said how the spirit was so large."

"Well, that was no coincidence," I said.

"I have got to admit it, Mary Francis. I was convinced."

"But weren't you disappointed that Ida Mae wasn't anything like Nora? I mean, she didn't even talk about any trips of her own."

"What *did* you mean?"

"Trips like Nora took. Trips through time and space."

"Oh, that. Your daddy never believed in any of that."

"But you believed in it, didn't you Gram?"

"Can't say as I did. I never had a real feel for it."

"You said it was possible."

"Anything's possible."

"What do you think about people who leave their bodies but just sort of hang around and don't go anywhere far off?" I asked.

"Can't imagine why they'd want to. Why'd anybody want to be so disconnected like that?"

This didn't seem like a good time to tell her about what I could do and about how I needed to learn to go farther so I could check up on Mama and Leland.

It had snowed some more while we were in Ida Mae's house. The fresh cover of white was puffy and dry and flew up from the toes of our galoshes.

"Looks like fairyland," said Gram. She wasn't doggedly moving ahead the way she had earlier. She lifted her feet slowly, looked at the sparkles as they drifted off, and laughed. "It's so beautiful, I could just die."

I'd never heard her talk this way before.

"Reminds me of when I was a very little girl in Michigan. A good snowfall was the most exciting thing that ever happened in our small town. Makes me realize how much I missed it when we were in sunny California."

"You don't want to go back to Beverly Hills?"

"I didn't say that, now, did I? I guess I'd go just about anywhere your father needs to be to make a living. That's what's different about me and your mother."

"Mama has dreams."

"Yes," said Gram. "I guess she does."

I expected her to say something else, something bad about Mama. But she just kept kicking the snow as if it were the most important thing she could think of to do.

Then she said, "I'm glad we walked to the party. I wouldn't have missed this for the world."

When we got back to the apartment, Daddy was asleep by the radio with the paper in his lap. Gram stopped to shake him awake, but I just went back to my room. I could see by looking out the window at the streetlight that snow was still blowing from the trees.

The séance had been a disappointment, yet I wasn't feeling sad. I felt like I'd learned something tonight, like maybe Nora had given me an answer after all but it would take me a while to decode it.

———

I was glad when school started up again because it was so quiet in the apartment now, and there were just so many games of king of the mountain I was willing to play with the Murphy twins. Since the time I'd thrown that snowball at Ike, they both seemed a little afraid of me, and I kind of liked that. I suppose they were still expecting me to say I was sorry, but I couldn't do it.

The kids at school kept talking about my skating accordion routine until I wanted everyone to forget it ever happened. (I did hope Mr. Gupper had changed his mind about my being in the band, but he hadn't.) It felt like such a long time ago. It seemed Mama and Leland had been gone for weeks instead of days.

Elsbeth, who I was planning on asking to be my best friend when I got back from vacation, had decided over the holidays to be best friends with Dolores. I didn't see why we couldn't all three be best friends, but when I told Gram, she said how three best friends made a triangle and a triangle meant trouble. She said that was why the twins and I could never play together for very long. Anyway, both girls had regular mothers who traded casserole recipes and could get excited about a new Electrolux vacuum cleaner. I didn't want to have to keep explaining about Mama, and I didn't think I was ready to share my secrets with anyone the way I suspected best friends did.

Most of the time I just wanted to be by myself and to

think about things. I hadn't had the urge to leave my body for a while now, and I wondered if I still knew how. The last few times it had been so very hard to come back that it petrified me. If I kept it up, would I always be able to return? I couldn't get rid of the idea that maybe, just maybe, I could eventually learn to travel to California by practice and the sheer strength of my will.

I was mulling this over on the way home from school, when I opened the storm door and Mrs. Feingold jumped out at me.

"Your grandmother's been calling down the stairs for you for the past ten minutes." Her look was almost reverent. "It's long-distance!"

"Thanks, Mrs. Feingold!" I called as I took the stairs two at a time. At the top, our door was open, and Gram had the receiver to her ear while she leaned out and urged me to hurry up. Before I had a chance to put down my books, she switched the receiver to my ear and thrust the long neck of the phone into my free hand.

"Mary Francis?" came Mama's voice over the wire. "Is that you, Mary Francis?"

"It's me, Mama."

"Well, I just couldn't wait until your father got home to tell you the good news. Here," she said. "I'm gonna let Leland tell you himself."

Pushing through a peal of static, Leland's voice seemed so small and distant it made me feel awful at first. But there was more excitement in it than I'd heard in a long time. He seemed happy — not overjoyed like Mama — but happy.

"I got the part, Mary Francis," he said. "I had that audition, and I got the part."

"That's just swell," I told him. "I'm really proud of you. Is it a big movie? Do you have a big part?"

"Mama can tell you the rest," he said, but I was desperate to keep him on the line.

"I miss you, Leland," I said. "Is everything all right? Do you miss me?"

"I miss you a lot, Mary Francis."

"Are you eating three meals a day?"

"We don't always have three meals a day."

"Do you feel good? Are you getting to bed early?"

But then Mama took the phone away and started explaining things about the new part.

"It's a really big part in a major MGM motion picture." She was sounding like a radio commercial. "Get this — the stars are Fred Astaire and Myrna Loy. What do you think of that? And it's gonna be in that new color process they call Technicolor."

I was flabbergasted. Gram was hanging on my every silence, and I turned to her and mouthed the names.

She slapped her hand to her mouth. "Just imagine! I'd have bet my bottom dollar nothing like this would ever happen to a Ferguson!"

"So you see," said Mama. "We made the right move

by coming home early." She was still calling it *home*. "I would have kicked myself if we'd missed this opportunity. This is it, honey. This is our big break!"

"That's wonderful, Mama," I said, trying to sound every bit as excited as she did. I was glad for Leland. I was happy that someone was paying attention to his talent at last. But I realized, with a sudden clarity that made me weak, that things were not going to get better for the family now, that the two little groups of us were going to drift farther and farther apart. Why, when Leland was as old as I was, he might not even remember me.

"Be sure to tell Daddy as soon as he gets in the door," Mama was saying.

"I love you, Mama," I said.

"Me, too, sweetheart. Me, too."

When I hung up the receiver, it felt heavy as lead.

"She's getting what she wants," said Gram.

"It's what Leland wants, too," I said.

"I wouldn't be too sure about that." But later on I heard her saying to herself, "Myrna Loy and Fred Astaire . . . just imagine!" and "Technicolor!"

"Well, see now, Ma," Daddy said when we told him the news. "Loreen was right all along. And it's like she always says, when you have a child with all that talent, you have this obligation to the world." But he didn't sound happy about it. In fact, he didn't even eat all his dinner and he went to bed before *The Green Hornet*.

Later that night Gram said, "It just makes me sick to see Forest mooning around like that. He's like a love-sick cow."

Lovesick. That was a good description for it. And it described the way I was feeling too — just sick to death in love with who we used to be and terrified of what we were about to become.

CHAPTER SEVENTEEN

MAMA'S LETTER CAME FIVE DAYS AFTER THE PHONE call even though you could see by the date on it that she wrote it that very day and sent it airmail. In it she told us some more about the movie, but Leland hadn't had a rehearsal yet so she didn't know much. At the end she asked Daddy for a little advance until Leland got his first big paycheck. She said how he needed some rehearsal outfits and how she had to dress the part of a successful agent. "You're going to get it all back in spades, darling," she wrote at the end. "Things are working out. They're working out just the way I planned."

"She's right about that," said Gram. She'd been reading over his shoulder. "But I can see the handwriting on the wall already."

"What handwriting?" I asked. Had I missed something?

"As Loreen would say, it's just an expression. What I had in mind is that it doesn't take some genius to figure out how she's sending the rest of us straight to wrack and ruin."

I was still confused. Mama's letter had seemed so

upbeat, but Daddy looked worse than he had after the phone call.

"I just don't know," he said, and he lowered his head into his hands. "I don't know where all this money is gonna come from."

Gram tried to stroke the back of his bald head. He let her do it for a few seconds but then pushed her away.

"You can't get blood from a turnip," said Gram.

"But she's made good on her end of the bargain, Ma. You have to agree about that. If I could just afford to bankroll her a little bit longer." He was sounding like Edward G. Robinson in one of those gangster movies. "If we just had enough cash to keep them both going until Leland's first paycheck . . ."

"That's just what she wants you to think, Forest. That's just the kind of bind she wants to put you in."

I hated to believe it, but I thought Gram was right. I thought Mama was asking for far too much this time.

"You send them money all the time as it is," I said.

"But apparently it's not enough."

"And it'll never be enough," said Gram. "What did you think would happen, Forest, when Leland got an opportunity? Did you think she'd just drop everything right then and there and come and live here?"

She started in with the usual kitchen clamor she made when she was good and mad.

"This is just the beginning," she continued. "No telling what she's going to need once Leland gets swept into this motion picture thing for good and all."

Daddy looked so helpless. His hands looked so useless against his head. I kept wishing he had enough hair to grab with his fingers and twist.

"What do you suggest I do, Ma? What can we do now?"

"You can sell the house, that's what. Why should those two keep rocking around in that big place as if 'Leland Lebec' were already a household name!"

"They've got to live somewhere."

"Well, not in some castle before she's even pronounced queen! She's making a fool out of you, Forest Ferguson. Why, I've got George's insurance money tied up in that house, too. She's making a fool out of the both of us."

Gram and Daddy were both real quiet after that, and I didn't know what was going on. But the next night, Daddy sat down after supper and wrote a long, long letter. He was still at the kitchen table when I went to bed. In the morning, I could see the stamped envelope with his briefcase by the door. I didn't need to see the address to know it was for Mama. Whatever it said, I was pretty sure she was going to be disappointed.

Three weeks later, there was a postcard in our box with a picture of our Beverly Hills house on one side and a write-up of all its particulars on the other. It mentioned the "roomy play yard," "inviting kitchen," and "proximity to beaches and fine shopping." At the bot-

166

tom in tiny print were the words "Loreen Ferguson: Realty Agent."

"You have just got to admire her," said Gram when she saw it. "Your mama doesn't miss a trick."

And it didn't take Mama long to find a buyer, even though it was supposed to be a bad market.

"No telling what she promised those poor people," said Gram.

When Mama called Daddy with the offer, she was all business and so was he. Daddy sounded like any stranger making a deal. He used words like *proxy* and *power of attorney*. He talked about closing dates and attorney's fees. When he put down the phone, he said to Gram, "Looks like a pretty good deal. We won't make much profit, but we've only owned the place for a year and a half, and you'll get out all you put into it. You've got to hand it to her, Ma. Loreen has a head for business."

"Monkey business," said Gram under her breath.

"What did you say?"

"I said you're always defending her. You'll be defending her until the day you die."

Daddy didn't say anything to that. He took his newspaper into the living room and snapped it open. I went in and sat on the hassock.

"Where are they going to live?" I had to ask this. They had to have a place to live.

Daddy lowered the paper and looked at me.

"She'll find a place, Mary Francis. You act like I'm kicking them out into the street."

"But she loved that house."

"I know that, honey. And I feel bad about it. I do. But we had to do something. The money for the things she wants just isn't there."

"Is she mad at us?"

"Right now she is. But one thing about your mama, she never stays mad for long."

He was right about that.

"It'll be like magic," came Gram's voice from the kitchen. "As soon as she needs something else, she won't be one bit mad anymore."

And Gram was right, too. But I had to stick up for Mama, though I couldn't think of much to say.

"She just has lots of good ideas," I said at last.

"She does have good ideas," said Daddy. "I wish I had all the money in the world and that I could give her all she needs for all her good ideas. But I don't. And I can't. Maybe someday she'll go off and find somebody who has and can." He kind of laughed, but he lifted the paper up so it covered his face 'cause what I think he really wanted to do was cry.

"She'll never do that," I said. "She loves you. Too much," I added. But just like always, I didn't know as I said it if it was really true.

———

"Looky here," said Gram when I got home from school the next day. She had the paper spread out over her sewing machine like she sometimes did when she took a break. "That movie, *Dancing Feet*, the one where Leland has that little part. It's at the Savoy in town tomorrow. Just imagine! At the Savoy already!"

"You said it wouldn't be released for a long time. You said not to plan on going to see it anytime soon."

"Well, I was wrong, now, wasn't I? I don't mind admitting that I was wrong. It takes a big person to admit it when they're wrong. The picture must have been so low-budget they put it in the theaters lickety-split to get their money back."

My blood fizzed up like soda pop.

"Wait'll I tell Elsbeth and Dolores! Wait'll I tell the twins!"

"And I suppose you'll want to go see it with your friends, too. I suppose I'll have to go alone."

"I think we should all go together the first time," I said. I was planning to go more than once. "Daddy, too. We should go tomorrow, when it starts."

"It's a school night."

"You mean you'd wait? I can't wait. Why should we wait?"

When Daddy heard, he didn't want to wait either. He said he wanted to see the returns he was getting on his investment. As he paid for the tickets, I heard him say to the girl in the ticket booth, "My little boy is in this movie, in the one called *Dancing Feet*."

"Really," she said. She popped her gum and didn't look up. "Next," she said.

He said the same thing to the usher, who remarked, "That's very interesting," before showing us to our seats with his flashlight.

The first movie of the double feature was already on the screen and we had to duck down to keep our shadows out of it. It was the second part of a boring Gene Autry serial that played in installments and that some of the kids at school had started seeing last week.

It was hard to sit through it, especially since we hadn't seen the first episode and didn't know what was going on. But even when *Dancing Feet* started to roll, we had a lot of waiting to go. At one point Gram whispered to me, "Are you sure this is the right movie?" There'd been lots of dancing feet so far, but none of them belonged to Leland.

About ten minutes later, just as it seemed that the story was winding down, there was this little speck of him tap dancing like crazy down this gilded highway in somebody's dream. At first you couldn't see much of him at all, but as he danced, he got bigger and bigger until he washed right off the screen. It was like he was there one minute and gone the next, disappearing the way stains were supposed to when you used Oxydol. I wanted to catch him as he flew off, but, of course, it was just an illusion.

"That's it?" asked Gram. "That's his big debut? Why, if you'd held your breath it woulda been over with before you felt the least bit desperate!"

"Loreen said it was a small part, Ma," said Daddy. "She never claimed it was anything else.

Gram snickered. "A star is born!" she said.

We called long-distance as soon as we got home. It was the first long-distance call we'd ever made, and Daddy let me talk to the operator and put it through person-to-person. He said how if he was going to splurge, he was going to do it right. Afterwards, it seemed like a silly idea because it could only be Mama or Leland, one or the other, who would answer.

I could tell Leland was surprised to get a call especially for him. And when I told him we'd seen his movie, he was kind of shy and happy at the same time and only talked a few minutes before he put Mama on. Turns out he and Mama hadn't seen it yet themselves, and Mama couldn't believe that it had come to what she called "your little burg" before it hit the big Hollywood theaters.

"I just hope he looks as photogenic as I think he will. Did he look photogenic?"

I wasn't sure what she meant. He looked like Leland. But the answer seemed very important to her.

"Yes, Mama," I said. "He looked just great."

"Well, that's a relief. Out here, someone can look absolutely perfect on the stage, but if they aren't photogenic, well, they just never make it, that's all." She seemed out of breath. "But you say he's photogenic, so that's a big relief."

I hoped that I was right.

Gram and Daddy wanted to talk to Leland so Mama put him back on the line and I handed over the phone. They told him all the right things — how great it was to see him up there and how fast his feet flew across the screen. But neither one of them asked to talk to Mama, and I guess she didn't ask to talk to them. I felt like the linchpin right in the middle of the family. If I let loose, everybody would fall away like separate strangers.

CHAPTER EIGHTEEN

MAMA'S LETTERS WERE ADDRESSED TO ME NOW, AND I suppose I should have liked being singled out like that, but I didn't like what it meant. When she wrote how she was packing things up to put in storage, I started thinking about all the stuff I loved that I hadn't seen in almost a year — my pink chenille bedspread and the flowered quilt, the white wicker rocker, the painting of a small pond and winding lane that she got at a yard sale and hung in the hall, Mama's own pink satin chaise lounge where I used to stretch out while she combed her hair and put on lipstick and rouge. The word *storage* sounded as lonely and cold as the word *tomb*. It was like she was putting parts of us into boxes and hiding them away. Would we ever see any of it again?

"I wish you were here to help me," she wrote in one letter. "Leland makes an effort, but he's just a little boy, after all. You were always so good at straightening things up and organizing. There's an awful lot of work here for one person."

If I could just be like Nora. If I only knew how to zoom into Mrs. Moran for one afternoon. Wouldn't

Mama be surprised when that lady offered to help? I could check to see that Leland was all right and Mama, too, and, of course, when all the packing was done and I knew they were both okay, I'd zoom back here and Mrs. Moran could go right back to being the neighbor they hardly ever saw.

It seemed perfectly logical that if I could travel out of my body at all, I should be able to extend my range. Well, even if Ida Mae Hanson's séance didn't give me the answer and Nora wouldn't or couldn't share it yet, it had to be out there somewhere. It might even be written down someplace. Why hadn't I thought of *that* before?

I started spending long hours at the library on my way home from school.

"You're turning into a regular grind," Elsbeth told me one day at lunch. "My mother says 'All work and no play . . .' Well, I can't remember the rest of it, but she says it isn't good."

But Gram thought it was a wonderful thing that I'd finally decided to become a better student. She said, "That's how you'll make your mark, Mary Francis, not in some make-believe fantasyland."

When my grades stayed about the same, she was confused.

"Where is all that information going when you spend all those hours soaking it up?" She asked that question right after I brought home my quarterly report card.

It was all going into a three-ring binder exactly like the one I took with me to class. Only I'd drawn a giant moon in ink on the cover of this one. This full moon had a friendly face on it and inside the binder were all the things I'd been able to find in books and magazines that had anything to do with spiritualism and out-of-body experiences. I even put in some of the history, like how there were lots of parents after the Civil War who wanted to communicate with their dead children, the ones who had been soldiers. That's when spiritualism became real popular, along with some of the practices, like picking auspicious times to get in touch with dead relatives, joining other people to call up the dead, and having an experienced medium make contact. (I don't think Ida Mae Hanson could have been very experienced. She talked way too much, she didn't go into a deep trance or anything, and she hadn't been able to keep Nora from fading away.) Some photographers said how they had photographed spirits coming and going, and they showed foggy-looking pictures as proof. A few magazine articles said it was all a hoax. There were a lot of books on the theory of leaving the body, but nobody had any recipes. What I needed was a kind of out-of-body cookbook with just what to do laid out in simple language.

When I couldn't unearth anything even remotely like that, I started applying common sense. To launch a balloon, you started in an open field far away from people;

when pilots like the Lindberghs flew in gliders, they took off from cliffs in California and other high places. Two important points: 1. Nobody who ever got anywhere (except Nora) took off from inside a building, especially some stuffy little apartment. 2. Every time my spirit had traveled, the sensation was of going up and up. So I figured if I started from a high point to begin with, I'd be bound to increase my chances of going farther. All I probably needed was more practice.

It had taken some time for me to come to these conclusions, to learn that there wasn't going to be any map and that I would have to trust my own inclinations. And then I had to decide on a place, someplace high that I could get to on foot.

It was the end of March, not really winter any longer, but not spring either. The days were blustery and cool; the streets were slick with dirty runoff from melting snow. Poke's Hill, the one near school where kids had taken their sleds and toboggans after a snowfall, glistened with all these tiny rivulets and smelled like wet earth and damp pine. After school, some kids still trudged to the top and tried to slide down on cardboard boxes or trash-can covers, but they always ended up a muddy mess far from the bottom. It was a long hike to the top, and it was probably still too slippery for what I had in mind. So I waited.

It wasn't until a sunny, almost dry day the beginning of April that I decided the conditions were right. Even though I knew I needed to follow through, my fear was so intense this time that I couldn't make myself hurry. I didn't go there right from school. I walked home, dropped off my books, and walked back slowly, telling Gram I was going to LeGrande's. I always stopped at LeGrande's to and from anywhere, so it was true. By the time I got to the school, it was completely empty of kids. There were a few teachers' cars parked in back, but there was no one in the playground or up on the hill.

I wore my galoshes in case there were still some mushy places, and I had on a heavy sweater since it wasn't really warm yet. Even with this spring weather, I was still wearing the blue hat to church, and I wore it now so I'd have something that I could see from far away and want to come back to. I thought of how I'd wanted to bring Leland up on this hill around Christmastime, but he and Mama went back before there was enough snow to use the Flexible Flyer he left behind. Daddy must have bought it for him thinking that he'd be staying for good; it made me sad. After they left, I had come here a few times with the twins, and we'd gone almost to the top so the three of us could ride their toboggan down to the bottom. I'd never actually climbed all the way to the top because there was a clump of trees up there that got in the way. This time I pushed through the trees and some very prickly bushes and came out at an open space at the very pinnacle. If I'd known how beautiful it was up here, I'd have come before today.

The other side of the hill fell away sharply toward the river below, which looked like a long twisting sash as it traveled into the valley. Everything was newly green and there was a soft haze surrounding each tree. Turning around, I could see the town, the mill, the triple-deckers on our street.

This place was so quiet. No people, no commotion, just clean, clear air and the earnest sound of phoebes that Mrs. LeGrande had told me were the first birds of spring. There was even a fallen log where I could sit so I wouldn't have to leave my body standing for too long. Even though there was a wonderful, safe feeling about being so high up and so far from everything, the fear that I might have a hard time coming back was still with me. I'd done it before, I reminded myself again and again. Even when it had taken all that I had to give, I'd done it before.

The leaving part had become too easy, though, and that frightened me as well, because I didn't want to take off before I was good and ready. So I waited. I looked out over the valley, drew in a deep breath, and waited. I thought of Leland. I thought of Mama. I thought of how they needed me. Of how we needed each other.

I probably should have eased more gently into all of that because this time, before I was at all prepared, it happened. Like a blink of an eye or a sudden memory, I could feel the material world slipping away and a peaceful rush lifting my inner self up and up. When I realized I was on my way, I tried to master my terror and will my spirit to speed up; I pictured the globe of the world at school marked with my destination and the arc I would need to travel to get to Beverly Hills. I was sure I was turning, gaining speed, going higher and higher. I was so excited about seeing Mama and Leland. I was certain I was on my way.

In spite of the fast and surprising start and a sense of going farther than I ever had before, after a while I gradually became aware that what I was really doing was heading straight up and up, and not up and out as I'd planned. And I had no sensation of traveling through time at all. After the first long thrust, I hadn't even moved on; I was hovering, just as I'd done before. Then I was being pressed into the sky as though it were a solid ceiling instead of infinite space.

The sudden sure knowledge that there was something beyond this ceiling that I would never be able to reach, the sense of the immensity of it, was so staggering I wanted to go back right away. And, though I could see the scene below in startling detail, I could also see, so distinctly it astonished me, that there was no reason in the world for me to be up here like this, that I wasn't going to be able to help anyone this way. But the force that had propelled and pulled me before was now thrusting me against an impenetrable horizon. I couldn't get beyond it or through it. I couldn't slip away from it no matter how hard I tried.

As though squeezed by an unseen hand, I felt like I was dissolving and had little will of my own. Compressed for what felt like endless hours against a small wad of sky, my sight traveled down the sun's rays as it set. The moon rose, and I followed its ascent and watched the way it polished the hill below with cold yellow light. Stars shone more brightly as the night darkened; clouds drifted back and forth across my plane of sight. Time after time I tried to escape the invisible hold. Time after time my spirit collapsed into itself and was forced to give up. If only it still took the same small wish to return to earth as to leave it! I could hardly remember what those first trips had been like.

I called on God. I called on Nora. I watched in horror as the moon began to fade and take on the appearance of a thin paper disk in a pale gray sea. It was almost morning, and Gram and Dad would have no idea where I was! Would I be here forever and ever?

I couldn't cry tears; I couldn't shout *Help!* There was nothing to do but continue to try and try to tear myself away. As I did this over and over, with as much strength as I could summon and with as little hope as was now left to me, and as I was getting prepared to stop trying, to just exist up here forever and ever and ever, there was a sudden rip, a tremendous sensation of falling, a fierce plunge to the earth.

I, Mary Francis Ferguson, the totality of myself, every single bit of me, was suddenly shivering in the damp air. I was getting up from the log, stretching and brushing myself off. I was climbing down the hill with careful, shaky steps.

Right afterwards, I didn't feel well at all. My skin was too tight. My eyes burned. My head ached. Every sound was too loud; every color too bright. I also felt like a failure and as despairing as if I'd lost the ability to see. It wasn't just that I needed practice. I knew now, without one single doubt, that I could practice for years and years and it wouldn't make any difference. Oh, I had the gift all right. But I didn't have Nora's gift. That was probably why she hadn't stuck around at the séance and why there hadn't been anything to decode after all. She had nothing to tell me that would help me in my situation, nothing that would help us all, and she knew it.

That left me with two choices. I certainly couldn't travel long distances in an instant to help people out the way I'd planned. But I could still take off when things got rough and hope that I'd always be able to return, or I could stick around and solve any problems in the ordinary ways I knew how to. That meant putting up with embarrassment sometimes, and sometimes confusion and indecision and all the things I couldn't think of right now that were ready and waiting to step out and confront me as they had before. It meant if I was going to help Mama and Leland, I'd have to really be there for them, *body and spirit*, and I'd have to find a way to do just that.

The lights were on all over the apartment when I got back. As I opened the door, Dad and Gram rushed at me with these awful, scared looks on their faces.

"I was about to call the police!" said Daddy. "I've been searching up and down all the streets of the neighborhood most of the night. Where in the world were you?"

I'm not exactly sure, I thought. But I told them, "I climbed Poke's Hill and fell asleep up there."

"You've never done anything like this before. What's gotten into you?"

"I was missing Mama and Leland," I said.

So far, everything out of my mouth had been true or nearly so.

"See! What did I tell you?" Gram said. "This is having as bad an effect on her as on any of us. The child feels abandoned." She pulled me close and held me. Her bathrobe was scratchy and warm.

Abandoned. That was true, too. It was the truest thing of all.

It surprised me when Gram suggested I take the day off to sleep. "You won't be able to keep your eyes open at your desk anyway," she said.

The day after that there was a letter from Mama waiting for me when I got back from school.

"You look kind of funny," said Gram when she

handed it to me. "Like you're coming down with something. I hope it isn't the flu. Mrs. Feingold had the flu last week and it knocked her for a loop."

"I'm fine, Gram," I said.

"What's your mother say?"

Did Gram know how annoying she was sometimes? I didn't even turn when I answered her.

"I haven't had a chance to read it yet."

I took the familiar light blue letter back to my bedroom and sat by the window, spinning it from one hand to the other. It had been so beautiful up there on the hill. Mama hadn't been here in the spring. She'd love how green it was. Now maybe she'd never have a chance to see it.

When I finally opened the envelope, the first few lines jumped out at me.

"Gram!" I called.

She came running with a bowl in one hand and a mop in the other.

"Mama wants me to come visit. She wants me to come in the summer and stay in the bungalow they're renting near Wilshire Boulevard."

"For heaven's sake! I thought you'd thrown up for sure."

"Do you think I can go? Do you think Daddy will let me?

"The train ticket won't be cheap."

I remember Mama wheedling for the round-trip fare

for her and Leland and how strapped it had made Daddy feel. But there was just one of me. I wouldn't even need to have a berth. I could sleep in my seat. I could sleep standing up in a parlor car if it meant a trip back to Beverly Hills and Leland and Mama.

"Let me think a minute," she said, scratching her chin on the end of the mop. "You've surely been away from your mother far too long. Just as a boy needs his father, a girl needs her mother, truth to tell."

She had said the thing about a boy and his father a million times, but I'd never heard her express herself like this on the subject of me and Mama until early yesterday. I didn't know what to make of it.

"And I just might be able to help you there."

Gram could help? What could she do?

She sat down on the edge of the bottom bunk and leaned forward. She smiled until I could see her dead blue teeth way in the back.

"I've been putting away quite a little nest egg since I saw the lay of the land at Christmas."

I wasn't sure what she meant by that, but I suspected she wanted to be ready to help Daddy out if he needed it.

"There was that slipcover I made for Mrs. Krakas and all those hems I let down for Mrs. Murphy. Sadie — Mrs. Feingold — had me do up a wedding veil for her niece." She arched her back and looked as pleased as a cat. "My potholders and tea cozies have been selling like hotcakes. Well, maybe not like hotcakes, but good enough to keep me going."

"I know that, Gram. But a round-trip ticket clear across the country will cost a whole lot of money." I didn't really know how much, but I had an inkling it was more than she suspected.

"Not for somebody twelve and under," she said as though she'd been thinking about this for a while. "It's a bargain for somebody twelve and under."

"I'll be thirteen by summer."

"Then we'll buy the ticket ahead of time."

Could we do that? Would Daddy agree? Was this really going to happen? We hugged each other. It wasn't something we did very often and it felt good. It felt so good.

If I was really going to travel back to Beverly Hills in the conventional way, in regular, clock-ticking time with my own body and spirit and brain, then Gram had been right all along. Anything could happen. And things, all kinds of things, could turn right around when you least expected.

CHAPTER NINETEEN

WE DIDN'T HEAR FROM MAMA VERY REGULARLY after that, and when we did, her letters were short and had few details. I couldn't wait to get out there and see if everything was all right.

I could tell Daddy was worried about me traveling so far by myself. He warned me about talking to strangers, about getting off at stops along the way, and told me I should keep part of my money in my sock and some in a special zippered pocket Gram had sewn into the hem of my skirt. He sent a telegram to Mama telling her just when and where I would arrive and spelling out in no uncertain terms that she should be there on time to pick me up. Though neither of us said it in so many words, we both knew she might forget, and he told me what to do in case I found myself alone at some point.

I left for the coast three days after summer vacation had started. It was just long enough to see that there were fun things planned for Hardenville, like Fourth of July fireworks and swimming lessons at the lake. But I consoled myself that there'd be time enough another year for those things. I wasn't completely part of this

186

place yet anyway. Before school ended, kids were making all kinds of plans for things to do together, and they didn't include me. Anyway, this summer I needed to be in Beverly Hills.

The trip was lonely and long. The scenes that flashed past the window were the same as the ones coming here, only in reverse. I knew now that I had to watch myself, that if I floated out into some wheat field or cattle ranch on a whim, I might never be able to find my way back, and an empty and useless Mary Francis would arrive at Union Station in Los Angeles on Friday at noon.

When we finally did pull in, I was so stiff from sitting that I wondered if I could actually pick up my suitcase and move down the aisle. Everyone staggered like zombies that had been asleep underground for a hundred years. The porter took my bag at the door and helped me down like I was a little old lady.

"Have a fine time in L.A., honey," he said.

I thanked him. But I didn't know if I was going to have a fine time or not. Especially if Mama forgot.

"Hurry up, Mama," I said under my breath as I watched dozens of other people who had just spent days of motion and silence with me connect with friends or relatives. For six days I had said "yes" and "no" and "thank you" and nodded at any question directed at me as if I had no language of my own. Gram said it would be safer that way, and Daddy had agreed.

Now I was dying to talk, really talk with someone,

with Mama and Leland, but they were nowhere in sight. I sat on my suitcase at the start of track six until my bottom went to sleep, and then I followed a stream of people into the lobby, where I was happy to find empty padded benches. But just as I sat down again, resigned to a long wait and running through in my mind what I should do if they never got here at all, I saw two figures struggling through the revolving doors. Leland was pulling on Mama, and Mama was looking up and all around as if she was lost in the woods or like she expected to find me in the very back corner of the waiting room.

"There she is!" yelled Leland when he spotted me. I jumped up and ran straight for him, picking him up and twirling him around like a stuffed bear. It wasn't as easy as it used to be, and he giggled so much, I was afraid he'd wet his pants.

"Why, Mary Francis," said Mama. "I can't believe my eyes. You're a good head taller. And your hair!" She held me away from her at arm's length.

"Gram sent me to the beauty parlor," I said, "so you'd be proud of me."

I was still having a hard time getting used to so much air on my bare neck.

"Why, isn't that just the sweetest thing! But I can't get over it, honey. You look like a debutante with that bob. I wouldn't have known you from the back."

"I'd have known you from anywhere," said Leland, and he gave me a big slobbery kiss.

And I'd have known them both, even though Leland was so much taller he came halfway to my shoulder and Mama looked thinner and milky white. The dress she wore seemed too big for her. It was one Gram had made for her about five years ago, and it was the first time I'd ever seen Mama wear something so out of style. It made her seem older and tired.

She picked up my suitcase, but I took it away from her.

"It's not far to the bus stop," she said. "Just outside the parking lot. We haven't had a car, you know, since your daddy left."

"But you never did know how to drive, Mama," I reminded her.

"I was planning to learn, Mary Francis. I really was. But then off he goes to that other job and leaves me stranded."

"You could have come along. He wanted you to so bad."

"I know, honey. I know," she said, patting Leland on the head for some reason. "Well, there you go sounding just like those two."

It was the first time I'd heard her refer to Daddy and Gram in that mean-spirited way. She laughed self-consciously. "What did I expect?"

"There's our bus," shouted Leland when we were still half a block away from it, "the one with the red sign in the window."

"Well, aren't you the one!" said Mama. "Yoo-hoo!" She called and waved at the driver while Leland and I ran ahead and asked him to wait.

Once on board, Mama asked for transfers and we found seats together at the very back.

"It's a long ride," Mama said, "until our change at Pico and Vermont. So get comfy. If there were just a train station nearer to where we live now, we would have been there to meet you in plenty of time."

I doubted if it would have made a bit of difference. But being with them again, I couldn't be mad. And now I had someone to talk to. By the time we'd transferred to the second bus and reached our final stop, I'd told Mama all the things that had gone on in Hardenville since the day they left, and she and Leland had filled me in on a few things about the movie set.

"That Fred Astaire is just as nice as can be. Not a bit hoity-toity, if you know what I mean. You can tell he likes children, though I've warned Leland he has to act real professional and not be a pest."

We had to walk down a couple of side streets after that. The skinny palm trees that I'd taken for granted in the past now stood out like telephone poles with green hair. My arm holding the suitcase was beginning to hurt, and by the time Mama said, "This is it!" I would have settled for anyplace at all.

The way Mama had been calling it a bungalow, I'd expected a neat little house like Nora's, but after we'd walked up the cement path and into a courtyard, I could see there were really several small places, all alike, like the cabins we'd rented on our trip east. Mama had a key to the one at the very back, which she said was more private than the ones in the front and had a yard. Inside, there were a few pieces of furniture that I remembered, but the rooms were too tiny to hold very much of what we'd had, and there was a stuffy, sour smell like dusty pea soup. I had to share a bedroom with Leland again, which was fine with me. He was so happy to have me there, he wouldn't calm down until Mama actually snapped at him, something I'd never seen her do.

"Well, honey," she said. "What do you think? It's not Beverly Hills, but we're still in the vicinity."

"It's fine, Mama."

"And the weather hasn't changed at all. Still more sunshine than any other state but Florida." She sounded like a travel ad and so uncomfortable that it made me feel that way, too. Leland had turned quiet and was slumped down in Daddy's old leather chair.

I reached over to tickle him.

"I'm not a guest, you know," I told him.

He laughed. "It feels that way."

"Well, I'm not. I'm still just your silly old sister." I tickled him some more until I made him laugh real hard.

"It's nice to hear him laugh," said Mama sort of sadly. "I thought he'd forgotten how."

I didn't know what to say. What was she telling me?

"I mean," she continued. "He works so hard at the studio. And then there's homework when we get back here."

"When will the movie be finished?"

"Oh, I expect they'll wrap it up by the middle of summer. Mr. Siegle — he's the director — says that more than likely it won't go much past the middle of summer."

"Then you can take a little vacation."

"Oh, no, honey," said Mama. "We're trying to line something up right now so that doesn't happen. We've got to get all the parts we can while Little Leland LeBec is still *little*, if you get my gist."

I didn't.

"You must have noticed how much bigger he's grown, even in the six months since we saw you last."

Of course I'd noticed it. Little boys were supposed to grow.

"I keep telling Mr. Siegle that he's just having a growth spurt, but he wants to know why Leland has to have a growth spurt on his time. Isn't that the limit! That man just makes me sick."

Mama pulled out a cigarette and silver lighter. I'd never seen her smoke before and was amazed to see her hands shake as she tried to light up.

"She smokes all the time now," said Leland. "Like the other grownups."

"I have to be on the set all day long with him," she said. "And I can tell you, all that waiting around, it gets old pretty darned fast." She flicked ashes into an ashtray I'd never seen that was already full. "You have to do something to wile away all those hours."

"Sarah Donlevy's mother knits," said Leland.

"I'm just not the type, darling," she said. "And it drives me crazy with her there day after day, click-clacking away to beat the band. Why, Mary Francis, you just can't imagine how nerve-racking that can be."

"What else do you do?"

"I talk with the other mothers or with the extras. We talk. And I try to make other contacts. You know, find out who's hiring juveniles. Things like that." She took a long drag on her cigarette. The room was misty with smoke. My head filled up and I started to sneeze.

Mama opened a window. "You'll get used to it, honey. It's funny what you can get used to."

There wasn't anything cooking on the stove at suppertime. Mama had been on the phone all afternoon trying to sew up what she called her little real estate deals until Leland started to complain that he was hungry.

"Well, of course you are," she said then. "There's a can of Campbell's tomato soup there, Mary Francis. Could you heat it up for us, honey? And could you make us some pimento cheese sandwiches to go with it while I make this last call?"

I'd had sandwiches for three days on the train — sandwiches for lunch and Gram's oatmeal cookies with raisins and dates for breakfast. When I finally had to break down and navigate the dining car, I'd ordered the cheapest thing on the menu, which was soup.

I wondered if she would have asked Leland to make supper if I wasn't here. I wondered if she always waited till the very last minute like this before deciding what they'd eat. When I opened the icebox, besides the jar of cheese, there was a dried-out package of bologna, a couple of eggs, and half a quart of milk. The ice was nearly gone and everything was slightly warm. An open can of chili had mold on top and smelled. There was a yellow head of lettuce way in back.

"You need to go to the market," I told her, "and you need more ice."

"You're absolutely right, honey. But until I get your daddy's check tomorrow, well, we'd just better hold off until then. You know what I mean?"

I checked the kitchen cupboards. Besides the tomato soup there was a carton of cocoa, some puffed rice, and a box of tea. There was half a loaf of bread on the counter. We wouldn't starve.

"Is it always like this?" I asked Leland as he watched me bump into things in the unfamiliar kitchen. There was hardly room enough to turn around.

"Not always. Just sometimes. When Daddy's check comes, or mine, she gets real happy. And sometimes she gets money from her real estate stuff. She goes out and buys us all kinds of things then. But sometimes a check comes and she doesn't spend it for a long, long time."

"What's the real estate stuff?"

"She rents apartments. She says you have to start out renting apartments. She says she's practicing up to sell Hollywood mansions."

I changed the subject. "Any kids around here?"

"Some. They play pickle or hide-and-seek after school, but Mama doesn't let me play if I have an early call the next day." He yawned, and it made me yawn, too. "Sometimes I'm too tired anyway."

"What's early?"

"Five o'clock."

"You mean a little kid like you has to be on the set at five o'clock?"

"Have to," he said. "It's my job."

He was sounding like a little man instead of a little

boy. His voice was flat and dry, without the pep it used to have. He chewed his fingernails.

"What about school?"

"I get tutored on the set by a crabby lady who isn't very good at arithmetic."

I laughed. How would he know that?

"Mama says that making the movie is learning experience enough."

There was only half a table to eat at — one leaf was folded down and the hinged part was up against the wall. There was no room to open it out. We squeezed into three folding chairs around it.

"Isn't this cozy?" said Mama. After a bite or two, she said, "What a good cook you are!" even though I'd just warmed the soup and slapped slices of bread together like anybody could do. "Isn't this just like old times?"

It wasn't anything like old times, but I was afraid of sounding like Gram if I disagreed with her. It was so much not like old times that I could hardly sit there and pretend. Leland ate his sandwich in a couple of gulps and asked for another.

"See," said Mama, "it's that kind of thing that's making you grow."

"I'm sorry, Mama," said Leland, "I just get hungry."

"Well, you're going to have to control your appetite, young man, if you want to stay in the movie business. You heard what Mr. Siegle said as well as I did. You know he's not going to be pleased at all if you grow as much as — what did he say — one more centimeter."

I wasn't sure how that translated into inches, but I knew this kind of thinking was crazy. I made another sandwich for him before Mama had a chance to tell me I couldn't.

"I just don't know what I'm going to do with you," she said as Leland wolfed it down and held up his glass for more milk. The bottle was empty, but at least he'd had the second sandwich.

"He's got to grow, Mama," I said. "That's what kids are supposed to do. They all grow up."

"Oh, I know that, honey. But does he have to grow up so fast? And does he have to do it now? I was all set to have cards made with 'Little Leland LeBec and his Dancing Feet.' You know? Like the title of his first movie? Now it's going to have to be plain 'Leland LeBec and his Dancing Feet.'"

"What's wrong with that?"

"It's not near as catchy. I mean, with the first one, you picture this darling little dimpled child. Right?" She looked around in this dreamy way. "He was going to give Shirley Temple such a run for her money." Then she got all serious again. "The second one could be just anyone. Anyone at all."

"Even Shirley Temple's getting taller. She's growing up."

"And you notice the parts for her are getting scarcer and scarcer? That's the way it happens. Overnight like that. You wake up one morning, and there goes your career!"

"Where?" asked Leland.

"Down the drain, that's where. All my hard work and your talent right down the drain."

CHAPTER TWENTY

IT WAS STILL DARK OUT WHEN MAMA WOKE US UP THE
next morning. Leland slid out onto the floor and began
to shuffle around the room. I pulled the pillow over my
head and went back to sleep for the two minutes or so
before Mama's hand began shaking my shoulder.

"I know it's hard, sweetheart, but you've just got to
get out of that bed. Unless of course you want to stay
home and read some of my magazines or sun yourself
out in the yard. I do want you to see what it's like on the
set, but I guess you can wait a day or so until you rest up
from your trip."

"No, Mama," I said. "I can do it. I can be ready." I
was still half asleep when I began stumbling around in
the dark looking for my underwear. I unpacked one of
the summer dresses Gram had made for me in a great
big hurry and I shook it out. "Is it really okay for me to
come along?"

"Sure, Mary Francis," said Leland. But Mama sort
of hesitated.

"Oh, I think it will be all right," she said finally. "I

mean, I never asked anybody, but I don't see why they'd mind. When we check in at the gate, I'll just tell them you're family come along for a look-see."

At 4:30 sharp, even before we had breakfast, a taxi pulled up outside and honked. Mama was quick to explain (in case I told Gram I suppose) how the buses didn't run this early, so a taxi was a necessary business expense. She said we'd pick up doughnuts in the commissary so we wouldn't have to waste time eating breakfast here.

Driving through the empty streets was exciting and strange to me, but Leland fell right back to sleep with his head against my arm. Mama asked to have the dome light left on so she could put on her lipstick and comb out her hair, and by the time we got to the studio gates, she looked fresh and shiny. She batted her eyes at the guard as if he was somebody special and so was she, and he didn't even seem to notice that I was beside her.

"There," she said far enough inside the gate so he couldn't hear. "That was easy enough. You're just going to have a great time, Mary Francis. You'll have the time of your life."

I was so excited by now I couldn't stand it. This was where movies were made. This was where movie stars worked. As a soldier brushed by me, I looked up into his face, expecting to see a famous person, but Mama whispered, "He's just an extra, honey." Other people in all kinds of costumes were rushing from one building to another or calling back and forth.

When we went across to the commissary for dough-nuts, I was sure I'd see movie stars. There was a girl about my age in a pinafore. She had makeup on and the strangest things on her feet — sparkly red shoes. And there was somebody who looked like Errol Flynn, but who Mama said was his stand-in. A beautiful lady with dark hair, who Mama said later was Hedy LaMarr, asked me to pass the sugar. For some reason there were a lot of little people hanging around. Mama said they were all extras in some fantasy about a wizard. As we were leaving, my personal favorite, Nelson Eddy, walked in.

"Do you realize how lucky you were to see any fa-mous people, Mary Francis?" said Mama. "This early in the morning you hardly ever see any stars at all. They're usually in their trailers or being made up."

Then she took Leland down to Wardrobe. He came out in little short pants that looked pretty silly, and he had lipstick on and rouge on his cheeks. Two little girls emerged looking more frilly but just as peculiar. They giggled together and ordered their mothers around, telling them where to sit and what they wanted and whining when they had to wait. I was glad that Leland didn't behave like that.

When Mr. Siegle came onto the set, everybody fell

silent. You could hear, "Good morning, Mr. Siegle," all over the place, as if God had arrived.

"Just stay out of Mr. Siegle's way," Mama whispered to me. What did she think I would do?

"Little boy," said Mr. Siegle, motioning to Leland. "Pay attention, little boy. Get over near the little girls."

"Two weeks on the set," muttered Mama, "and he still doesn't know Leland's name."

"Where are the stars of the movie?" I asked. I was dying to see Fred Astaire.

"They usually come in late."

I couldn't stop looking for them, but I started to get caught up in all the confusion going on around me. How were they, how was Mr. Siegle, going to straighten everything out and make a movie out of it? Right now the cameramen were sitting back in their chairs and smoking. The stage crew was hefting props around. Somebody kept turning lights on and off until I felt dizzy.

"How long do they keep this up?" I asked Mama.

"Keep what up?"

"This fooling around."

"Oh, they're not fooling around, honey. I thought that, too, at first. But everyone is just doing his little part to get ready for today's shoot. Sometimes we do two scenes. Sometimes only one. It's such a hot day, I don't expect they'll get too far."

When Mr. Astaire arrived, the pace really picked up.

He got right to work practicing his routine, and it wasn't long before the choreographer began rehearsing the children and everybody was dancing. At one point the *tap-tap*ping got so loud it was giving me a headache. One of the other mothers started knitting like crazy, one did crossword puzzles, and Mama brought out her cigarettes. In the middle of all this hubbub, Mr. Siegle sent Leland back to Wardrobe.

"Get Wally to flatten down that curly top of yours," he said. "We need to take those inches off somewhere or you'll tower over the little girls."

Mama nudged me. "See what I told you! He makes a crack about Leland's height every chance he gets."

I didn't see why Leland couldn't be taller than the girls. I didn't see why he wasn't just right.

While everybody waited for Leland to return, practicing steps and things, Mama introduced me to one of the other mothers, who said to me, "Your brother's a natural. Fastest feet in the business. Nice little boy, too."

"See," I said to Mama when we went to find seats. "People are beginning to appreciate him already."

"That's just Mrs. Donlevy," said Mama. "What does *she* know? What kind of connections does *she* have?"

"I thought it would make you happy."

"What will make me happy is when somebody on the top gives Leland some notice, not somebody's mother." She lit another cigarette, sat down, and started jerking her foot in time to the music. "If Leland and her daughter were after the same part, she'd change her tune, believe me."

As soon as Leland came back, the dancers began rehearsing their new routine again, with the choreographer running the kids through all the steps. Leland's hair was plastered down into a shiny helmet that made him look like a doll instead of a live boy. It didn't even fly around when he twirled.

"Mr. Siegle," called Mama during a lull. "Surely you don't want my client to look foolish in this sequence. Surely you don't want him to stand out from the rest."

"Madame," said Mr. Siegle, "all I want is that your . . . er . . . client look short. Is that too much to ask? We hired a short little boy. If the only way we can keep him that way is to plaster the hair, then we plaster the hair."

Mama turned red-faced and feisty.

"But it's his curly hair that makes him who he is — his curly hair and his dimples and his fast little feet."

"Madame," said Mr. Siegle, "it is his contract that makes him who he is. And the contract gives me absolute authority when it comes to what he shall wear and how he shall look. I suggest you read clause number three, Section A, part three, and I suggest you allow me to do my work and your . . . client to do his."

I was surprised when Mama didn't answer him back. She looked as if she might pop, though, and she turned to me and muttered, "Isn't that the limit!"

"It *is* Leland's job, Mama. You told me so yourself."

"And it may be his last job if he comes off looking like some freak."

"But he's photogenic," I offered, remembering what had been so important to her before. But it was the wrong thing to say.

"A photogenic freak!" she said.

"Don't worry, Loreen," said a mother who seemed to know her better than the other one. "It'll look different on the screen. It always looks different on the screen." She reached into a big sack and pulled out a Thermos. "Have some coffee, dearie. Have an apple. Try a cookie."

"No thanks, Erma," said Mama. "Erma, this is my daughter, Mary Francis. She's very talented, too."

"Oh, isn't that nice. What do you do, honey?"

I didn't know what to say.

"She's a skater," said Mama, "a fabulous skater. Why, you'll probably be seeing her in some Sonja Henie Technicolor spectacular one of these days."

My mouth wanted to hang open so badly, I had to press it shut with all my might.

"Isn't that swell how both your children got talent," said Erma. "Parmalee is the only one out of my six with even an ounce. To tell the truth, she's not much of a dancer, but just look at that gorgeous little face. It melted Mr. Siegle's heart. It melts everybody's heart." She looked at me closely and smiled. "It's good you can skate."

I glanced over at who I suspected was Parmalee, a little girl with beautiful brown eyes, bleached blond hair, and two left feet.

"The way I understand it," said Mama when Parmalee's mother had moved closer to the action, "the camera focuses in on Parmalee's face then cuts to somebody else's feet. Isn't that the limit!"

I agreed.

"But it's also show biz," said Mama. "It doesn't have to make sense, it just has to make entertainment. I'll admit to you, though. Sometimes I feel as if I've fallen down the rabbit hole like what's-her-name—like Alice."

"But it's worth it, right?" I asked. I didn't know what I wanted her answer to be. I didn't want to think that we'd put up with the long separation and what Gram called "our unnecessary hardships" for nothing. On the other hand, I wanted Mama to discover that there might be a good reason, a really good reason, why the movie business wasn't everything she'd dreamed it would be and that what *we* had to offer was a whole lot better all along.

"Worth it?" Mama asked as if she was in some kind of daze. I noticed all at once that though her face was the same as always, her eyes looked old. "Oh, I don't know, Mary Francis. Sometimes I just don't know."

CHAPTER TWENTY-ONE

WE TOOK THE BUS HOME AND DIDN'T GET BACK TILL dinnertime.

Both Mama and I realized at the exact same minute that we still hadn't been to the market and now there really was nothing in the house for supper.

Mama sighed long and loudly and threw herself into Daddy's old chair. "There's a little Italian restaurant we can walk to if I can ever get up again."

I wouldn't have believed anyone could become so worn out from just waiting around if I hadn't been exhausted, too. Leland, who had done all the work, was still going strong.

"He'll fold right after supper," said Mama.

And he did, almost falling asleep on his feet on the way back from Luigi's. Only a year earlier, I would have been able to carry him home.

The spaghetti had been spicy and filling, and as soon as we got back to the bungalow, even though it was still light out, we all collapsed into our beds and didn't wake up until Mama's alarm went off at 4:00 A.M.

This time I turned onto my stomach and mumbled, "I'm staying home!"

Mama tiptoed over and put some money on the night table.

"Make a list for yourself, honey," she whispered. "You know what we need. I'll leave the key on the dresser."

After that, I went with them or stayed home just as I pleased. The first day had been exciting, but it had been long and boring, too, just the way Mama had described it. And there was plenty that needed doing in the bungalow. The kitchen floor was so sticky it all but glued the soles of our shoes. There was a washer with a wringer that Mama had hardly ever used, a pile of dirty clothes in her bedroom, and empty clotheslines outside the back door for drying things. I wasn't much of a cook, but Mama couldn't have been happier if I'd been some French chef. I guess having supper ready when she and Leland got home reminded her of how it had been with Gram in the kitchen, even if I didn't know how to bake wonderful things or follow recipes.

"Cooking is a talent, too," she kept saying, probably to keep me at it, but I was glad to see that she was pleased about something. So much of the time now she seemed too tired to care about anything at all.

When Daddy called to find out how I was getting along and didn't ask to speak to her, it just broke her up.

She cried so hard she got the hiccups and had to lie down.

The times I did go to visit the set, I'd get as furious as she did at the way Mr. Siegle treated Leland. Leland only shed tears over it a few times, and when he did, you could see he was trying not to make any noise. If you didn't know him as well as I did, you might even have missed it.

It was so pitiful that once when Mr. Siegle called him "our big little twinkle-toes," I decided I couldn't take it anymore. Somebody had to stand up for Leland if he couldn't do it himself.

"And you're a big baboon!" I yelled at Mr. Siegle. It was the worst thing I could think of on short notice. I jumped up and ran over, ready to sock him in the nose, but acres of assistants and secretaries got in the way and held me back.

"Who is that large, impertinent girl?" He spit the words out. "Get her off this set. Get her out of here! Get her off the lot!"

Mama came over and took me away, all apologetic, which made me sick. Why was she willing to put up with what this ogre kept saying to Leland, with how he was hurting his feelings?

Later I thought about how I really wanted to bop him one even though I knew it might wreck everything for Mama. I'd decided by that time that this dream of hers — the movies, fame and fortune — had nothing to do with what Leland wanted. He was a kid. He wanted what kids want. He wanted to dance in the same way that he wanted to do things like play ball and kick the can, and he wasn't getting to do any of that.

Mama ranted on about Mr. Siegle that night and how she was going to report him to the Screen Actor's Guild, how that was the "proper avenue of complaint" and not the "physical confrontation" that had occurred to me. She did imply, without coming right out and saying it, that she admired the way I'd stuck up for Leland and that she wished she had the guts to do it, too.

I was afraid to say what I was thinking, but I had to blurt it out. "If it's so hard, Mama, and if Leland's already too tall for all you had in mind, why not quit while you're ahead?" It was such a Gram thing to suggest, and I expected her to be furious.

"And sit back and watch Ma and Forest gloat over my failure! Admit that we've wasted a year of our precious time on this earth, that I've kept Leland away from his father and me away from my husband and daughter all this time for no good reason?"

She sighed as if she was about to die, and I felt so sorry for her that I picked up both her hands and held them. "People make mistakes, Mama."

Her eyes opened up like little rivers. She bent her head, and her tears began to splash into the soup.

"This one's a doozy," she said. "If I knew any way out of this predicament with my pride intact, I'd take it, Mary Francis. You know I would. Leland needs his father. I need him, too."

"And me. Do you need me?" I had to ask.

"Why, of course I need you, sweetheart. That goes without saying."

"No it doesn't, Mama." I jumped in deeper. "Both of us, both Daddy and I, maybe even Gram, we need to know that we're important, too."

Mama was flustered. "Why, I thought—I mean, I was sure—it just seemed to me that it was understood. I thought you knew that we were all making sacrifices, myself included." She put her arms around me. "That time I almost lost you to the river, I wanted to throw in the towel right then and there. I did."

"It's not too late," I said.

Leland had jumped down and was playing marbles on the bare floor.

"You mean I wouldn't have to work anymore? I could stay here and play with Mary Francis?"

"Not so fast," said Mama. "Think about it this way: What are we going to do about the fact that Leland still has all this talent? Nothing's changed there."

"And it's not going to go away, Mama. What did Fred Astaire do when he was a little boy? I'll bet he played ball and skated on the sidewalk. I'll bet he ate whatever he felt like eating. You said it yourself. Just plain Leland LeBec and his Dancing Feet. That could be anyone from two to fifty-two. It could be anyone at all."

Mama surprised us the next morning by saying she was taking us to see the La Brea Tar Pits. Mama said how we all needed this vacation day and how she had planned what we'd do long before I came. It wasn't as though I'd never seen the La Brea Tar Pits, but she knew it was a favorite place of mine, and it was free. Also, we could walk there now. It was just the way I re- membered it — the sky so blue and bright it seemed fake, and the pits all dangerous and black, like looking into the pupil of some monster eye.

We stayed up on the paths and the grass, away from the edges. Mama said, as she always did, how there should be fences for safety and little signs to tell you more about what it was you were looking at. Daddy had told us once how all these prehistoric creatures fell into the pits over time. Their bones were preserved forever and ever, and scientists were still digging them up for study. Some of the pits were so close to the street, I al- ways wondered why people just walking along didn't slip in sometimes. I wondered aloud what it must have been like for those big animals to fall into all that tar and not be able to climb out.

"I know exactly how it felt," said Mama. "Just the

way I'm feeling now. Sometimes you dig a hole so deep for yourself that there's no climbing out." She started to cry again.

"Is it all my fault?" asked Leland.

"No, sweetheart. Of course it's not your fault. It's nobody's fault." But right away she took that back. "It's my fault for having all those big ideas."

"Ideas are good," I said. "I had a really big idea once. Some time I'll tell you about it. And it didn't work out, at least not in the way I'd planned."

"That's a shame."

"But I learned a lot. I learned a lot of things that I never could have learned any other way."

"That's true isn't it? Going through hard times, trying things out, it makes you understand the important things."

"I'll try to stop growing if you want," Leland said.

Mama laughed. She did it with her head back like she used to a long time ago.

"You shouldn't do that," she told him. "I must have sounded insane. I've just been so worried and so confused. I haven't talked to Forest in such a long time. I feel divorced."

"You're not divorced, but he's scared to death you might find somebody else who can afford your ideas."

"Did he say that? What a thing to think. What a precious thing to say!"

We didn't call Daddy right away. Mama said she had to work it all out, but I was pretty sure now that she'd come up with the right answers. And, of course, Leland had to finish the movie.

"He has a contract, after all," said Mama.

I wondered how hard this was going to be for her — giving up all the industry talk, not seeing the glamorous stars anymore, not hoping for a star of Leland's very own.

"It's like Gram said once," I told her. "It isn't as if 'Leland LeBec' is already a household name."

She seemed startled and got a faraway look in her eyes for a moment.

"A household name. Now wouldn't that have been something! Wouldn't that have been something else!"

Daddy drove out to pick us up in the middle of the summer, taking his entire two-week vacation to make the trip both ways. By then the movie was finished, he had already made an offer on a house, and Gram had agreed to pitch in again on the down payment. He said it wasn't as big or grand as the one in Beverly Hills, but it was on a hill and you could see the river. He'd made arrangements for our things in storage to be moved whenever he gave the word.

"Gram is keeping the home fires burning," he said.

"She said she thought we should have some time for ourselves."

"Why, isn't that the sweetest thing?" said Mama. "And Forest, I never saw you as such a take-charge type before. I like this about you, Forest. I really do."

There was so much she liked about him now that Leland and I could hardly get their attention away from each other. They held hands even while they ate.

"I hope you understand, darling," I heard her say once, "that this doesn't mean I've changed. Opportunities abound all over this great land. I can't approach the world with blinders on, now can I? I've got to be myself." Then she added, "And I have a good feeling about this move to the eastern seaboard. What better place to develop my talents for real estate? I don't know whether you realize it, Forest, but I do have a decided bent for it. And then, of course, after Leland gets through these awkward years, we can try the movies again. I can just see it. A young Tyrone Power who can dance. Won't that be something! Won't that be the living end?"

Daddy was in such a mood, and Leland's growing up was so far away, I was sure he'd have agreed with Mama about anything. I was glad I was going to be around for Leland no matter what Mama decided to do later on. He needed someone to look after him with a little more care than she was able to muster. And with all of us together again and Mama right there where I could find her, I might not want to take off the way I had in the past. Just knowing that I could, it was like Leland always knowing that he could dance and sing or like putting something to simmer on the back burner that you'd probably never get around to serving for supper. For it was suddenly as clear as day that Mama and Leland hadn't come back to us — that the family hadn't come together again — because of my gift but because I'd learned to do without it.

"Just imagine," Gram said one day when the subject of Nora came up, "what Mary Francis could have done with a gift like that!"

F   Collins, Pat Lowery.
Col
         Just imagine.

                    35793000276369
$15.00

DATE			